Dear JoAnn—

Enjoy the chase!

Barbara Siebeneick

SILENT SORROW

Barbara Siebeneick

Silent Sorrow is a work of fiction, any resemblance to people living or dead is purely coincidental.

Copyright 2019 Barbara Siebeneick

Book design & assembly by Foglia Publications,
Prescott Valley, Arizona

Printed in the United States of America.

Sincere thanks to Mieke Toland whose knowledge of Art Therapy helped me understand the psychological impact of being abused and abandoned. Her support and encouragement mean the world to me. Many thanks to Detective Kimberly Zook of the Monterey Police Department for her insights into the police department and other procedural information. Chief Bosuns Mate Joe Vizzi of the Coast Guard was essential in helping me understand how the Monterey Coast Guard Station works with the local police.

1

"**911** What is your emergency?"

A male voice answered, "There, there's a dead woman on the beach! She's just lying in the sand."

"Are you sure she is dead?"

"When I turned her over, I checked for a pulse, but there wasn't one. Her eyes were just staring at me, but there wasn't any life in them. They were weird looking. Like undercooked eggs. Sort of, glassy. I'll never forget it."

"Sir, where are you? Are you still with the her?"

He answered with a shaking voice, "Yes, I saw a man pulling her from the water, but he ran away when he saw me. I had to decide if I should chase the man or look to see if she was okay. I decided to stay with her."

"What is your name?"

"George Edwin."

"Where are you? Which beach?"

"I don't know what it's called. It's the beach down near the volleyball nets, across from Lake El Estero."

She said, "We'll send a patrol car and an ambulance

down there to check it out. Please wait there until they arrive. Don't touch anything." *It doesn't sound like a prank call, but you never know. Four-thirty in the morning is awfully early to be taking a walk on the beach, especially in this rainy weather.*

***

Detective Brad Evans walked between the few looky-loos along the beach, stepped under the yellow crime scene tape, and up to Officer Tom Kent who was talking to an older man. He realized the rain had stopped, so he folded his umbrella and approached Kent.

I still can't get over seeing Kent where Jimmy should have been. He was so young. He survived the Gulf War to die in Monterey. My stomach lurches every time I remember how Jimmy died from poison that was meant for me. If it weren't for my sister, Bea, finding me in time, I would have died too. Shaking off the feeling of remorse, Brad approached Kent.

"What do we have here, Tom, is she dead?"

"Yes, definitely. The Coroner is over with the body checking out the scene. The forensic guys are done with all their pictures."

Nodding toward the person standing by him, Officer Kent said, "This is George Edwin, he called 911 to report the body." Mister Edwin's light-weight wind breaker was zipped up to his chin and a hat with the "Red's Donuts" logo was on his grey hair. He was hunched against the cool, coastal air.

"Hello Mr. Edwin, I'm Detective Brad Evans from the Monterey Police Department. Would you please tell me what happened here?"

"I already told the officer, but I guess I can repeat it. I was on my way to work, I work at Red's Donuts, and I have to go in early to start baking before our regular customers start showing up. Anyway, I looked over and saw a guy pulling something out of the bay. When I got closer, I could see it was a body. I yelled at him to ask if he needed help, I thought he was rescuing someone. Instead, he looked up and ran away. He had a bike laying on the bike path and he jumped on it and took off. I didn't know if I should follow him or check on the person he was pulling from the water. He was already out of sight so I went to check on the body."

With a tremor in his voice he added, "It was a woman. She was soaked to the bone, I gently turned her over and when I moved her hair off her face, her eyes were open and just staring past me. It was the worst thing I've ever seen. I checked her pulse, just to be sure, but there wasn't one. Then I called 911."

George let out a long sigh and lowered his head. "I've never seen a dead body before, except at funerals, and then they've been all fixed up. This was different. So different. I'll never forget the way her eyes were open, but you could tell her soul had moved on. It almost looked like a mannequin."

"Did you touch anything else or move the body?"

"No, the guy that ran away had already pulled her out of the water and I didn't do anything more than I told you; I turned her over, checked her pulse and moved the hair out of her face."

Brad asked, "Did you get a good look at the man who ran away?"

"It was dark, but it was a full moon and I got a pretty good look at him. He was Hispanic. Shorter than me, so I'd say about five eight, brown hair, jeans and a rain jacket. Maybe a hundred and twenty pounds. He was skinny. He had a dark baseball cap with some kind of logo on it. Not a sports team, I would have noticed that. It looked like something I've seen before, but I can't place it. If I remember, I'll tell you."

"Would you be able to recognize him again?"

"I think so."

"Can you guess at his age?"

"I don't know, maybe somewhere between eighteen and twenty-five. These days everyone looks young to me!"

"Thank you for your help. Officer Trent will get your contact information and I'd like to see if you can work with our sketch artist to make a drawing of what he looked like. Here's my card and if you think of anything else, give me a call."

"Can I leave for work? Those donuts won't bake themselves. Stop by later and I'll have a bag for you. I guess cops still like donuts, don't they?"

"We certainly do, but we aren't allowed to take gifts. Save us a bag and we'll pay for it."

"Now, as soon as we get your contact information you can go. Please don't discuss this with anyone. You know how rumors fly around Monterey. We don't want the suspect to know you got a good look at him."

Brad went over to look at the body. He bent down on one knee and then turned to talk to the coroner. Doctor Jared Parker was about five feet five and one hundred sixty-five pounds. Brad could see his sandy, thinning hair over his stooped shoulders. "Hey Doc, what have you got? Was it a drowning?" Brad lifted the corner of the sheet covering the body.

Doc Parker raised his metal framed glasses to look at Brad. "Hi, Brad. It's just a guess without a more thorough examination, but she has a severe head wound that may have been the cause of death. The cold water might change my estimate of how long she was in the water, but I would think it was probably a couple of hours. Her body temperature was at seventy-five. I didn't find any identification on her. It looks like she is in a nightgown, so there weren't any pockets. No underwear and no jewelry of any sort either. I'll see if I can find any identifying marks when we get her back to the morgue in Salinas."

Brad looked down at the woman lying in the sand. *She must have been very pretty with that blond hair and slim build. That simple nightgown doesn't seem to fit her though. No jewelry, shoes, or even any signs of underwear. Was she getting ready for bed and fell overboard or was there something more sinister in her death? Who are you? Where are you from? What brought you here to our shores?* Brad silently said a prayer for her and for himself that he might bring her soul peace. He stood and stretched his broad shoulders while wiping a hand over his head.

Brad could see the water starting to lap at her feet. "Was there any sexual assault?"

"I'll take a swab at the morgue, but chances are, the water washed everything away."

'Thanks, Doc. I'll be over tomorrow to watch the autopsy, okay? The tide is still coming in and I guess you'll want to get her bagged before she gets wet again."

2

B ea Oakley approached the doors of San Carlos
Cathedral in Monterey. She had been thinking about
last year's murders and wanted to light a candle and say a
prayer for Jimmy Williams, Frank Jacks and the Cardinal.
She shuddered as she remembered finding the body of
Cardinal Charles Barrows in the Cathedral's crypt. Every
time she went to Mass, she remembered him lying there,
surrounded by blood. She hadn't forgotten the murder of
Frank Jacks, Jimmy Williams and the attempts on Detective
Brad Evans that followed.

*All that death over some old, forgotten, treasure. How
could someone kill the Cardinal and two others? I still find it
hard to believe that so much evil exists. Maybe I should say
a prayer that the killer will find salvation in prison. Doesn't
it say something in the Bible about gaining the world and
losing your soul? At least the killer didn't get away with it
and Brad is alright now. He was extremely lucky to have
survived both a poisoning and knife wound. My brother is
strong, but that was a lot for anybody. I don't know what I
would have done if he had died.*

Brad Evans and Bea were twins and their bond was

extremely close. They looked a lot alike and had grown even closer as life had thrown them challenges. They were both five feet ten inches tall and had the broad shoulders of former swimmers. Although they were in their forties now, they had kept active and healthy. It was a shock for Bea to see her healthy brother in the hospital after the attempted murder and poisoning.

Bea stood by the holy water font near the entrance, shook out her umbrella, and left it against the wall. In the last pew she noticed a little girl curled up in a ball, fast asleep.

She must be waiting for her parents. I'll just slip by and not wake her.

Moving toward the front of the old church, she stopped at the large statue of Our Lady of Sorrows. It was one of her favorites. Dressed in black with a handkerchief in her hands, Bea liked the way the statue depicted the sorrow of Mary as she stood at the foot of the cross. The tear running down her cheek made her seem so real. The statue from the 1800's was beautiful, but dirty. The cloth dress was so fragile that she couldn't be cleaned. Occasionally, someone would replace the white handkerchief with a clean one, but it was amazing how fast the traffic dust and fumes would turn it brown again.

Most statues look so cold and emotionless that it's hard for me to identify with them, but this one speaks to my heart. To me she represents the sorrow of all women. I remember when my boys were little, I would come here to look at her and remember that she was a mother too. It would give me strength to deal with the little problems of being a parent. Thank goodness my boys were pretty easy, but all kids have their moments. I can't really picture Mary having problems with Jesus, but she must have felt a lot of pain over his crucifixion and death.

I wonder what happened to the silver crown and sword that pierced her heart? I've seen a picture of them in the Heritage Center. Somewhere in the archives there must be a note about it. Maybe when I have some leisure time, I'll check it out. Hah! As if that will ever happen!

Bea proceeded forward to the transepts where rows of candles were glowing along a side wall in the dimly lit church. Putting a couple of dollars in the offering box, she lit three candles and spent some time remembering and praying for Cardinal Charles, Jimmy and Frank.

As she returned to the entrance, Bea noticed that the little girl was still on the pew and was shivering in the cool church. Drawing closer, Bea noticed that the child was wet. Wetter than being out on a rainy day would cause. She saw that the small, slender, child was watching her.

Bea moved closer. "Hello, are you okay? "

The little girl jerked and shrunk away from Bea.

"Where are your parents?"

The child looked at her with sad, fearful eyes.

"You are shivering, why don't you put on my coat for a while. Do you mind if I sit here with you?" The child shook her head slightly, so Bea took off her coat and gently placed it around the child. Then, she sat on the pew about a body's width away from the girl. "What is your name, sweetheart? My name is Bea. Are you waiting for someone?" The child just stared at her with a blank look.

"Well, why don't I just sit here with you until your parents come. Would you like something to eat?" Bea searched around in her purse until she came up with a granola bar and a small bottle of water. The child shyly took them and then ate and drank as if she was starving. Finished, she gave Bea a shy smile.

"I'm glad you liked that. I wish I had more to give you. You know, I have two boys. They could always eat more of what I gave them. We used to say they had hollow legs! They are grown up now and in college, but I always hoped I'd have a little girl too. Do you have any brothers or sisters?"

When the child still didn't respond, Bea began to wonder if she couldn't talk or had some other kind of handicap. *Who would leave a child like this, alone and wet, all by herself?*

***

Father Mike O'Hanlon entered the church through the massive wooden doors. Bea always thought that he looked like a young Harrison Ford with his crooked smile, rugged looks and sandy hair. He was a sensitive and loving shepherd of his parish. Bea enjoyed the mix of deep thoughts and folksy humor he added to his sermons.

"Hi Bea, how are you doing and who is this lovely young lady with you?"

"I'm fine, but I'm not sure who she is, Father Mike. I found her here, cold and wet, and thought I'd try to talk to her. She seems alert enough, but she hasn't said a word."

Father Mike sat down on the pew in front of them and turned so he could see the little girl. When he got close, the girl shrank away from him and moved closer to Bea.

"Don't be afraid darling, Father Mike won't hurt you." Bea put an arm around the child, drawing her close to make her feel secure. She brushed the wet, blond hair out of the girl's face.

"Hi, I'm Father Mike. What's your name?" Not getting a response, Father Mike continued, "That's okay, you don't have to tell me now, but maybe later, when we are friends. Did you know that this is my church? Well, actually it is God's church and I just get to live here and take care of it.

I have a house next door that is a lot warmer than in here. Would you like to go there? Bea can come too."

The girl looked up at Bea and, when she was reassured that she would be safe, she nodded her head.

"Are you okay to walk? It's only a little way."

The girl nodded and held Bea's hand as they crossed the small parking lot between the church and the rectory. Father Mike led them inside. "Bea, why don't you take her into the bathroom and dry her off bit. I'll find something warm that she can wear and set it by the door. Then I'll set a pot of water on to make some hot chocolate. Meet me in the kitchen when you are done."

Shortly afterwards, Bea and the child walked into the kitchen. She had on a T shirt with WWJD (What Would Jesus Do) across the front and a huge bathrobe that Bea had tied up, as well as she could, to keep her from tripping. The sleeves were also rolled up several times. Bea had dried and combed her hair and the child looked warm and cozy.

They sat down at the old, wooden, 1950's table. The child pulled her bare feet up so they were snuggled under the bathrobe. Father Mike was pouring some hot water in three cups and adding some instant hot chocolate to it. "I like my hot chocolate with lots of marshmallows. How about you?"

The child just looked at him, so he gave her one to eat. When she just stared at the marshmallow, Bea took one and ate it to show her it was okay. Slowly, the child reached out and put a marshmallow in her mouth. A look of pure joy lit up her face.

"Well, I guess you like them. In that case I'll put two in your cup. Be careful though, it may still be hot"

The child picked up the mug and wrapped her hands around the outside. She took a small sip. Again, a smile spread from ear to ear like she'd never tasted anything so heavenly.

"Do you like that? Drink slowly and I can make you another one later."

"Father, she seems very hungry. Can I make her a sandwich or maybe some eggs? Do you want anything, Father?

"No thanks, I already had breakfast, but go ahead and use anything you can find in the refrigerator. We don't really cook here anymore. It's not like the old days when every rectory had a cook and housecleaner. Mostly, I get by on the generosity of parishioners who own restaurants. They even cater to my diet."

"Now that we are friends, I wouldn't deny you a good meal, would I child?" Father Mike looked at the girl and asked again, "Can you tell me your name? Where are your parents?" Once again, the child just stared at him mute, confusion and fear in her eyes.

A few minutes later, Bea came back with a plate of scrambled eggs, bacon and buttered toast. She placed them in front of the little girl who looked at her as if asking permission to eat.

"Sure honey, that's all for you. Eat as much as you want."

The child reached into the plate to pick up the eggs with her hands. Bea stopped her and showed her the fork next to the plate. When she just stared at them, Bea showed her how to use the fork and knife. Bea looked over her lowered head at Father Mike, sending him a quizzical look. Silently asking, what child doesn't know how to use a fork? After finishing the meal, the girl's eyes began to close and eventually, she fell asleep at the table. Father Mike gently gathered her frail body into his arms and laid her on the couch in the next room. He covered her tenderly with a blanket.

Bea and Father Mike went back into the kitchen where they could talk, but could still see her. "Bea, I think this child has been abandoned. We need to call the police," Father Mike whispered.

"Poor thing, she is exhausted. There is definitely something wrong with her. When I was changing her, I noted some serious bruises on her body. She is also very thin. I could see all her ribs. I wouldn't be surprised if she hasn't been abused as well. I'll call Brad to see what we should do." Brad Evans was Bea Oakley's twin brother. She had helped him last year after she found the body of Cardinal Charles Barrows in the Crypt of San Carlos Cathedral, and he was always the first one she turned to in times of trouble. They looked as much alike as twins could without being identical. Beyond their similar appearance, they were also alike in spirit. Warm, honest and fair-minded they faced life with a positive outlook.

"I'm sure he will know what to do."

3

Detective Brad Evans pulled into the driveway and walked into the Rectory.

"Father Mestres?" Father Mike said.

They met in the hallway. "Hi Father Mike, it's just me. Are you expecting the ghost?"

"No, I just say that whenever someone comes in unannounced. I haven't seen him myself, but the story is that he is still here."

"So, the story of him haunting the parish is true?"

"There are a lot of stories from the older parishioners. Enough of them that I can't discount that it's real. Some say he sets up for Mass. Others say they have seen him walking around with a candle. I'm not saying I believe or disbelieve. Whatever, he is a friendly ghost and has probably moved on to his final reward by now."

"I hear you've found a little girl. It seems like yesterday I was here talking to you about the murder of the Cardinal."

"Come into the kitchen. As I recall, you did more than just talk to me about the murder." Father Mike rubbed his wrists like they still hurt from the handcuffs.

"I'm so sorry about arresting you for the murder, but everything was pointing at you. Bea has made sure that I have suffered for doing it. I thought you would have forgiven me by now. Isn't that part of your job description?"

"Come on, I was just kidding you. Of course, I forgive you. That's part of my job, but I'd do it anyway. If anything, that little stunt endeared me to the parishioners. I'm not sure it did the same for you though."

"You are right there. I got the stink eye for months whenever I went to Mass. You may be Irish, but the Italian mommas have adopted you as one of their own."

Leading Brad into the kitchen, Father Mike pointed to the small, blond, child who was restlessly sleeping on the couch in the living room. She would jerk and cry out as if having a bad dream.

"Bea found her asleep in the church and I brought her here to warm up and get something to eat. She was soaking wet and shivering. I'll warn you that we haven't been able to get her to say anything and there are possible signs of abuse."

Brad glanced in at the girl and turned to Bea, giving her a brotherly hug. "Hi Bea, have you found another mystery for me to solve? She seems harmless enough."

"Yes, she is a sweet little thing, but she is afraid of

everything. I found bruises on her when I changed her into the robe and T shirt she has on. I saved her dress in a bag for you, but it was soaked through, so I don't know if you will find anything on it to help you. She seems to have bonded with me, but she is still shy around Father Mike."

"Since she is still asleep, Father Mike, can you show me where you found her in the church?"

"Well, Bea found her, but I can show you where they were sitting when I came in."

***

Brad and Father Mike went into the Cathedral and Brad inspected the pew where the little girl was found. The seat was still wet and there was a puddle of water on the floor. Brad reached a finger into the water, smelled it and then, tasted it. *Hmm, salt water. Father Mike told me she was very wet when they found her. I thought at first, she must have been out in the rain, but this is too much water and rain wouldn't be salty. Could she have been in the Bay?*

Brad picked up his phone to call the office. "Hi Tom, can you send a team over to San Carlos Cathedral? I know you are busy with the murder this morning, so get here when you can. We have, what looks like, an abandoned little girl. Has anyone been looking for a lost child? No? Then we also need to call Child Protective Services to tell them we are taking her to the hospital."

Brad put away his phone and the two men went back to the Rectory. As they walked in, they could see Bea and the child sitting in the kitchen having another cup of hot chocolate.

"You have created a hot chocolate monster, Father Mike. When she woke up the first thing she did was go in the kitchen and lift up the cup for a refill. Of course, with marshmallows." Bea smiled and gently ran her hand through the child's hair.

Unfortunately, when the child saw Brad, she jumped and spilled her cup. She shook with fear as she looked at the mess.

"Well, it looks like we have a little spill, doesn't it? Said Bea calmingly. "My mother always said, 'Don't cry over spilt milk', or chocolate in this case. We'll have that cleaned up in a jiffy. Come here child and give me a hand." Bea handed her a rag and the two of them cleaned up the mess. Bea wiped off her mug, gave her a hug and started to make a new cup with extra marshmallows.

"This is my brother, Brad. You don't need to be afraid of him. He is a policeman and is going to help us find your parents."

The child looked at him warily, and stayed close to Bea.

Brad sat down across from her at the table. "Hi there, are you enjoying the hot chocolate? I love it too, especially with marshmallows. My name is Brad, what's yours?"

"Okay, you want to keep that secret for a while. Do you know where your home is?"

When he still didn't get a reply, Brad took a piece of paper out of his pocket and started folding it as he talked. The child was following what he did with a sideways glance. "I want you to understand that we are all friends here. You know Bea and Father Mike and I hope you will be friends with me too. Do you think Bea and I look alike? Well we do. That's because we are twins. That means we were born at the same time. Interesting isn't it?"

The girl became more intrigued as Brad's paper formed itself into a crane. With a couple of last moves he pulled on the paper crane's tail and the wings began to move up and down. Brad slid it across the table and let the girl try to make the wings flap. "You have to do it very gently or the paper will rip. Can I show you how?"

When she nodded, Brad went around the table and took her hands to show her how to work the origami crane. After a couple of tries, she was able to do it on her own and she looked at him with shining eyes.

"So, now we are friends, can you tell me your name?"

When she still didn't reply Brad started to become concerned. *Maybe she can't talk? That'll sure make my job harder. But I heard her making noises when she was asleep. Who is this child?*

4

These people are very nice. Man told me, though, not to trust anyone. The lady is kind and the man with the funny collar, Father Mike, was good to me too. I've never had hot chocolate before, or marshmallows. They were really good. Father Mike dresses a little like the man who led me here, to his church. I'm not sure what a church is, or God, but it's better than where I came from.

DON'T TRUST ANYONE! She could hear Man's voice in her head like he was still there. I want to talk to the lady, Bea, but the words won't come out of my mouth. I'm afraid. Whenever I talked to a stranger, Man would hit me and then hit my mother for not controlling me better. Is he waiting outside for me?

I was trying so hard not to be noticed. Whenever Man saw me, he would find some reason to hit me, so I tried really hard to become invisible. When the first man with the funny candle led me to the church, I curled up in the dark corner in the back, thinking no one would see me there. The man in black sat with me for a while, but he left when Bea came in. He just, sort of, disappeared.

Man told me there were bad people outside our boat

and we couldn't let them know we were there. That made me afraid, but Man was a bad man too. I couldn't believe it could be worse. So far, everyone I've met has been really nice.

I don't want to ever go back there. What if the police return me to him? Man told me to never, ever talk to the police, but Brad is a policeman and he seems nice. If I tell him about Man and Momma, I might have to go back to Man. So, I'll have to not tell him anything. These people are much kinder than Man ever was. I hope he never finds me. The child's eyes teared up as she thought of going back to Man.

"Oh my, are you okay? Don't cry. You are safe here and we will make sure that you are taken care of," Bea crooned, pulling the child closer. She stroked her cheek and took a tissue to dry the tears rolling down the girl's face.

Bea look sideways at her brother, "Brad, if you find her parents, I hope you throw the book at them. Who could hurt and abandon such a sweet little thing?"

"Believe me, Bea, there's nothing I hate more than a child abuser. They will get what they deserve when I catch them, and I *will* catch them."

"I'm going over to check on how things are going at the church. Can you stay here with her for bit more? She seems to be attached to you."

"Of course," said Bea, "I would love to stay here with her. I'll just call Pat to let him know where I am." Bea gave the girl another hug and pulled out her cell phone to call her husband.

"Hi, Pat. It's me. I'm over at the Rectory with Father Mike. There was an incident at the church and I have to stay here for a while. No, I didn't find another body. It's not like bodies are dropping in front of me every day! It's a little girl who seems to have been abandoned. She trusts me and seems to be afraid of men, so Brad asked me to stay with her while they check things out. No, you don't need to come over. I think another man around here might make her even more nervous and afraid than she is already. I'll be home as soon as I can. Love you, bye."

Bea dialed the number of the thrift shop run by the church. It was on the next street and did a nice business run by donations and the help of volunteers. The money they made went to help finance the Catholic school next door. "Hi Chris, is Branches open today? I'm over at the Rectory with a small girl that needs a change of clothes. She's about five years old and really slim. Can you find a complete outfit; underwear, shoes, shirt, pants, socks, etc.? I'll pay you for whatever you bring. I know your thrift shop needs all the money you can get to stay open."

It was only a few minutes before there was a knock on the

door and Chris stood there with her arms full of clothes. "I brought over a couple of outfits, in case some of it doesn't fit. Take what you need and return the rest when you can. Is this the little girl?" Christine noticed the child hiding behind Bea's legs. "Aren't you pretty. What's your name?"

"She is a little shy and hasn't told us her name yet. Thank you so much for the clothes, I'm sure we will find something that fits. Bea tried to slowly lead the woman out the door, without being rude. "Please don't tell anyone about her, okay? We don't yet know where her parents are."

"My lips are sealed. Working in a thrift shop, we meet all kinds of people and many of them don't want anyone to know they are down on their luck. Your secret is safe with me."

***

Bea laid the clothes out on the couch and held them up to the girl to see if they were the right size. "Well, isn't this a nice t-shirt! Do you like unicorns? I think these jeans will also fit and Chris even brought over a sweatshirt and jacket for you. These socks and sneakers seem about the right size too. What do you think? Should we try them on?"

The girl nodded her head and looked like she couldn't believe her luck. They went into the bathroom and emerged a few minutes later with a complete outfit that fit perfectly.

The child twirled around slowly, trying to look at her new clothes from all sides.

"Well, Father Mike what do you think? These clothes certainly fit better than your old t-shirt and bathrobe. I'll take them home to wash them for you."

"No need. Tomorrow is my laundry day anyway and I can just throw them in with the rest. But, what did you do with the little girl from the church and who is this beautiful child?"

The girl giggled and looked at Father Mike with a big smile. She took Bea's hand and looked at her adoringly.

"Every woman and girl likes new clothes once in a while and these seem to have worked wonders," Bea commented, smiling.

5

Eliott James slammed the newspaper onto his table at the Paris Bakery. Customers all around him looked up to see what the noise was about. Elliot glared at them until they lowered their heads and appeared inordinately interested in their coffee and croissants.

Eliott's thin, pocked marked, face wasn't attractive at the best of times and the anger he now showed made him look truly frightening. *I can't believe it. There it is, right on the front page of the Monterey Herald!* The caption read, "Body of Woman Found on Del Monte Beach." The article stated that an unidentified woman had been found on the beach early this morning and they were trying to find anyone who might know her. From the description, Eliott knew they were talking about the woman he killed.

How many dead women, who look like her, could show up on the local beach? She must have washed ashore after I threw her overboard from my boat. The blow I gave her should have killed her. We were far out in the bay when I threw her overboard. I was sure she was dead. How could she have landed here? Well, at least no one knows her here. Where did I pick her up? I think this one was in Newport, Oregon.

I wonder what happened to the kid? The seas were rough that night and she didn't know how to swim, so I imagine she drowned. Good riddance. That kid was a pain in the butt. Always hungry, always crying. I thought I had knocked some sense in her, but then she goes and jumps off the boat after her mother. I hoped I was rid of both of them.

I don't think they can tie me to the body. We never married, so there aren't any legal documents, and after I picked her up off the streets, I never let her leave the boat. Who knew she'd get pregnant right away? I should have drowned the kid when she was born, but the mother put up such a fight I figured I could use the kid to keep her quiet.

I'll finish my business here in Monterey and then I'll set out to sea. Maybe I can pick up another sweet young thing to replace the one who died. I was getting tired of her anyway. I may not be the best-looking guy around, but I know how to woo the ladies.

6

B rad told Bea that they needed to take the girl to get checked out at the hospital. "If she is bruised, there might be other injuries too."

Brad turned to the girl and took her hand, "Come on sweetheart, we are going to go for a ride to see the doctor."

The child violently jerked her hand out of his and ran to Bea. She hid her face in Bea's side and held fast to her body with her thin little arms. "That's okay dear, Brad won't hurt you. Remember, he is my brother and a friend. You can trust him."

The girl only clung to Bea more tightly. She was shaking in fear and her eyes began to water.

Brad looked at Bea, "Do you think you could go with us? I don't want to force her."

"Of course!" Taking the girls arms from around her and turning her face up toward her own, Bea asked, "If I go with you, would that then be okay?" The child nodded her head and wiped her tears with the back of her hand. Bea handed her a tissue to blow her nose and then led her outside to Brad's car.

***

The short drive over the hill to the Community Hospital of Monterey (CHOMP) took less than ten minutes. One of the things Brad liked about the Monterey Peninsula was how close everything is. Unless there was a big tourist event like the Concourse de Elegance or a golf tournament in Pebble Beach, the traffic wasn't too bad.

As Brad, Bea and the child entered the Emergency room, he checked in at the triage desk. They took seats in the waiting room among all the other sick and injured patients. Soon, a nurse came out and ushered them into an exam room. Bea could hardly walk because the girl had wrapped herself so tightly around her leg. They were led to a small, sterile room with a bed, one chair, a lot of lines attached to machines and a monitor on the wall. There was a glass door and a curtain that could be pulled around the room for privacy.

Bea gently removed the girls tightly wound arms from around her leg. "Come on darling, let's hop up on this bed. We'll slip you into a gown and then the nice doctor will come in to look at you. Don't worry, you'll get your clothes back. See, I'm going to put them in this bag for later. There's no need to be afraid, he will be very gentle and not hurt you. Brad and I will be here the whole time."

A nurse came in with a warm blanket and several

nurses came in to take her temperature, draw blood and hook her up to an IV bag. As each thing was done, Bea explained what was happening and why. The child was hesitant, but bravely endured everything. Even inserting the line for an IV bag didn't evoke a sound from her.

Finally, the door slid open and a tall, slim, athletic looking, woman doctor, walked in. "Brad, look, it's Doctor Velk! Remember how she took care of you last year?"

"How could I forget? She saved my life, not once, but twice! How are you doing Doctor Velk?"

"Well, Detective Evans, are you here to be patched up again?"

"Please call me Brad. No, actually I've brought you a little girl who was found at the Cathedral. We haven't had any calls at the station about a missing child, so we think she may have been abandoned." He turned his back on the bed and quietly added, "Bea said she also noticed a lot of bruising on her torso."

Walking toward the child, the tall, willowy doctor said, "Well, Brad, let me see what we have here. Hi, my name is Doctor Velk and I am going to examen you for a minute. Can you turn your face this way with your eyes wide open? I'm going to shine a light in your eyes and look at them. Very good. Can you open your mouth very wide and say AHHHH? I'm going to put this stick in your mouth and look at your throat. Excellent. Now I am going to listen to your heart with my stethoscope. I promise it won't hurt. Would you like to listen to Bea's heart first? Just put this part in your ears and the flat part on her chest." The child's eyes widened as she heard Bea's heart beating. "Now it's your turn. Sit real still while I listen. Good job!"

"I'm going to look at your legs and then lift up your gown to look at your tummy, your private bits, and your back. Okay?" Doctor Vlk paused when she looked at her back, concern crossing her face. Finishing her exam, she turned to Brad, "Can we step outside for a minute?"

"There is extensive bruising on her back. Some of it is fading and some looks new. Those are signs of ongoing abuse. She is extremely underweight as well. I want to run some X-rays to look for any broken bones. There doesn't seem to be any signs of sexual abuse, thank God. Has she mentioned to you who might have done this to her?"

"That's part of the problem. She doesn't talk. The sound she made when you checked her throat was the first purposeful sound she has made. We know she understands what we say to her, but she never says anything."

"That's another common occurrence for children who have been abused. They are so traumatized that they are afraid to talk. They have a difficult time trusting other people. I don't see any structural reason she can't talk, but I'll have an Ear, Nose, Throat doctor look at her."

"She seems to have built a bond with my sister. Can she stay with her while you run the other tests? I am working on a murder case and need to get back. Social Services should be here soon. By the way, we still haven't had that dinner I owe you."

"You don't owe me anything. I was just doing my job. Anyone on duty that day would have done the same thing. Since you aren't my patient any more, I won't be breaking any ethical boundaries by eating with you. Give me a call when you have some time and we will work out a date." Flustered, she added, "I don't mean a date, I mean a day we can get together for dinner."

"I'll send you the report on the child's condition. I'd like to keep her here for a couple of days to put some weight on her and give the bruises time to heal."

"Great, I'll call you. I don't mind if we call it a date!" Brad smiled broadly at the blush that covered her face.

"I'll just tell Bea I'm leaving and then I'll be off." Turning back, he added, "Wait, I don't have your phone number. Can you put it in my phone?" They exchanged phones, added the numbers and, smiling, he walked back into the exam room.

"Bea, I have to get back to the office. Doctor Velk is going to take some x-rays and then admit her for a couple of days."

Bea glanced at the sleeping child, "Poor little thing. I'll stay with her a long as she needs me. Would you call Pat and tell him what's going on?"

7

B rad drove over to the Sheriff's office in Salinas. After checking in, he made his way to the autopsy room. The Pathologist and two assistants were already waiting for him. The body of the young woman was lying under a sheet on the table. There was a bright light shining on her and a tray with various knives, saws, and picks. Brad thought she looked peaceful. *Thank goodness she won't feel what is about to happen to her.*

After everyone exchanged greetings, Doc Parker removed the sheet and began to make a "Y" shaped incision on her chest. He inspected the ribs and then cracked them to look at the heart and other organs. He removed the heart and organs, weighed them and had the assistants take samples. The whole while he was doing a verbal commentary of his findings for a recording. "The heart looks healthy, but the ribs show substantial evidence of previous breaks. Some of them are only partially healed."

Next, the pathologist had his assistant remove the stomach and pour out the contents. "There isn't much here. She must not have eaten for a while before her death. Her body weight is below average for her height and age, so the lack of food doesn't surprise me. Either she was anorexic or she was underfed. I don't see any of the normal signs of anorexia and, together with the many injuries, I would say she was being abused."

The pathologist made x-rays of her arms, legs and head. "Again, I see evidence of breaks that were left to heal on their own, dating back several years to more recent. There are also signs of sexual activity, with bruising and tears, indicating rough sex or rape. No semen was found. Probably washed out in the bay. She had at least one pregnancy. This poor girl has been through hell."

Brad was feeling queasy from the smells and sights, but he knew the worst was yet to come. The pathologist examined the head wound and then took a saw and removed the top of her head. Brad had to take a deep breath to steady his nerves as the pathologist reached in and removed the brain and put it in a metal bowl.

"The head wound is substantial, and would have knocked her out, but she didn't die from that. The head wound would have incapacitated her enough though, to make it difficult to swim. The cause of death was drowning. There is sea water in her lungs and that would not be there if she wasn't breathing."

Brad was glad the autopsy was over. *I can barely make it through one and these people do it all the time.*

"Do you think she hit her head accidentally or was it from a blow?"

"From the design of the fracture in the skull, I would say that she was hit, and not by accident."

"Thanks for your work, doctor, I certainly don't envy you your job."

"Well, I guess people can get used to anything. I look at it like a puzzle to be solved and a gift to the families who want to know how and why their loved ones died. Speaking of which, we didn't find any other identifying markers on her. No tattoos, no moles or scars that would be identifiers. We took an impression of her teeth, but they hadn't been taken care of for quite a while, so dental records may be hard to come by. I would put her age at between thirty and thirty-five. For now, we are listing her as a Jane Doe."

"Did you do a DNA sample?"

"Yes, but you know how long those take to get back. It will be a couple of weeks at least and, with the holidays coming up soon, it might be even longer. The labs are always backed up. I'll see if I can put a rush on it."

"Well, as soon as you get it, I'd like to know. Thank you, we'll keep in touch."

***

The breaks, bruising, and malnourishment sounds very much like the little girl that Bea found. They also look a lot alike, with their blond hair and blue eyes. I don't believe in coincidence. I wonder if they are related somehow? I guess we will have to wait for the DNA results or for the child to start talking. Should I show the woman's picture to the girl? No, that would be too traumatic. I'll just have to wait until her DNA comes back and then see if it is a match.

8

When Brad pulled up to the single-story Monterey Police Department, he saw Tom Kent getting out of his patrol car. His tall, hulking, body was hard to miss. His uniform stretched tightly across his chest and biceps and his flat stomach showed that he worked to keep fit. *I bet he played football at one time.*

"Hi Tom, how did everything go at the beach?"

"Fine." He said while hiking up his heavy utility belt, "We canvassed the beach for anything unusual, but it was hard to sift through all the cigarette butts, coffee cups, straws, candy wrappers, condoms, dirty diapers and other waste that people leave behind. We also talked to the people who were standing around watching us work. I didn't see anything unusual in the crowd's reactions or in the garbage we found. There were a few footprints, but the tide had washed away anything that might have been there earlier. George Edwin pointed out which footprints were his and which probably came from the man who was seen pulling her out of the water. The rest were from our people."

"Tom, would you take a couple of uniforms with you and check with the businesses around there and some of the homeless who hang out in that area? Maybe someone saw something or someone. At that time of the morning I doubt if anyone was around or awake, but it's worth asking. There were a few spectators when I got there, so it is possible that someone else was there earlier. I just got back from the autopsy and that poor woman has been through hell. I really want to nail whoever did this."

"Me too. Ever since my brother was murdered, I get so angry when I see another senseless death. Brad, did you see the article in the Herald today? I didn't notice the press there, but someone must have told them there was an unidentified woman found on the beach. I can't believe they got it in the morning paper already. Usually it takes a couple of days to get anything in print."

"No, I was at the hospital with an abandoned child. Well, it's too late now to stop it. Maybe someone will come forward with information on who she is."

***

Brad entered the police building and worked his way back to his desk. He pulled out his computer to write up reports on the two cases he was working. *I didn't know about Tom's brother. No surprise that he is so intense when following up on crimes.*

I wonder if the child and woman are related? It seems too coincidental that two women who look the same, have the same signs of abuse, and were both in the bay, don't have something in common. My bet is mother and daughter. The woman is too old to be her sister and the pathologist said she had given birth at some time.

9

Bea was still at the hospital. She had asked Doctor Velk if it would be alright if she stayed overnight with the girl. They brought her a blanket and pillow and she spent a rather uncomfortable night in the chair in the child's room. Bea looked up as a red jacketed hospital volunteer entered the room.

"Hello there. I'm Carole, one of the hospital volunteers. I heard there was a new child in here and I thought I'd bring over some crayons and a coloring book for her." She placed them on the table next to the bed and turned toward Bea. "Are you her mother?"

"No, just a friend. She won't be here too long so they allowed me to stay with her until she leaves."

"Isn't that nice. It can be scary and lonely to be here all alone. Especially for children. Well, I have to be off. I hope she likes the coloring book. If you'd like a newspaper, I can bring one by on my way back."

"No need, my husband is bringing a change of clothes and the paper from home. Thank you anyway."

Bea looked over at the bed and noticed that the girl

was already coloring in the book. "What a nice job you are doing with your coloring. May I see what you have there?"

The coloring book dealt with children who were in the hospital. Some in wheelchairs, some on crutches, some with bandages, and some just lying in bed. The child showed her the page she had colored of a child with a smile on her face, lying in a hospital bed. She had colored the hair yellow and the eyes blue.

"Why that looks just like you. Are you smiling too?"

The child looked up at her with sparkling eyes and a big smile.

Bea looked at the happy child and asked. "You know, I would really like to know your name. Can you tell me? No, well how about if I pick out a name to call you for now? Cinderella? No. Brunhilda? How about Girl Who Colors? No, too long. You know, I always wanted a little girl. If I had one, I was going to call her Claire. Would it be okay if I called you Claire for now? Super. Now Claire, what do you think we are going to have for breakfast?"

"Claire looked at her for a moment and then drew a picture of a cup. The liquid inside was brown and there was something white on top."

"Is that a cup of hot chocolate with marshmallows? You certainly know what you like. If we don't get one with breakfast, I'll go to the café and get you one. Deal?"

Doctor Velk came in the room to see the two smiling at each other. She took Bea aside. "Well, she is looking better already. Bea, I got her x-rays back and there is evidence of several, poorly healed breaks in her bones. Luckily, none of them were severe and she is still growing, so I don't think there will be any permanent damage. I've arranged for a doctor to come in today and check her vocal cords to see if there is a physical reason she doesn't talk. I'd like to keep her here until tomorrow and then release her to Bates Eldridge Family Advocacy Center. She needs more fluids and I want to get her weight stabilized. They are used to working with child victims and will do an interview before releasing her to Child Protective Services. If no family member comes forward, she will probably go into the foster care system."

"Oh no, Claire is too sweet to go into the system."

"Claire?"

"I got tired of calling her girl or child so she and I agreed to call her Claire, for now."

Doctor Velk looked at Claire and she nodded her head in agreement.

"I'm not sure if that is a good idea, but who am I to say? For now, officially, she is listed as a Jane Doe."

"You know, I just completed the training to be a foster

parent and I have extra room at home now that my boys are away at college. Do you think I could become her foster parent?"

"Bea, that's something I can't answer. You'll have to check with the powers that be. There is a long process to be certified. If you need a letter of reference, I'll be happy to give you one. I've seen how comfortable she is with you."

"I already finished the foster parent program. Since the boys went to college, I find I have extra time on my hands. I love having children in the house so I looked into the program and decided I wanted to do it. My husband, Pat, agreed too."

10

Brad picked up his cell phone from his kitchen counter and typed in a couple of numbers and then deleted it. He walked away and went back to pick it up again. He started to dial and then deleted it again.

What is the matter with me? I'm acting like a teenager. It's just a girl. I've been out with lots of women. It's just dinner, not a real date. I know I trusted Maria and she betrayed me, but Christina Velk is different. She is a doctor. She has helped me and has been always nice.

Brad took a deep breath, picked up the phone and dialed again. This time he held on while it rang. After just a couple of rings, Christina picked up. "Brad, what a nice surprise! Did you call to check on the girl?"

"Well, actually, no. But how is she doing?"

"A couple of days in the hospital has done wonders for her. She was dehydrated and is already looking better. It will take more than a couple of days to regain a normal weight, but she has a good appetite and she doesn't need to be hospitalized to gain weight. She still isn't speaking, which is a concern, but the Kinship Center knows how to work with children like her. Her sleep is also a concern. She is very restless and often jerks awake as if she has been scared by something. What child wouldn't be afraid after being abused and abandoned? Anyway, I will be releasing her to the Kinship Center today for them to do an evaluation."

"That's good. I know Bea has become very attached to the little one. Uh, um, I really called to see if we could arrange that dinner I owe you."

"Brad, you don't owe me anything. I was just doing my job. Any doctor on call that day would have done the same."

"You said that before, but I find it hard to believe. Anyway, not all the doctors are as pretty as you! Are you available on Friday?"

"Well aren't you the flatterer. I am available! I have the whole weekend off, so any day you pick."

"Okay, do you like Mexican? I was thinking of going to the Whole Enchilada in Moss Landing. It's a little farther out and not as many people will know me, or you."

"Are you trying to hide our date?"

"Oh no! I just hate to eat when everyone is nodding my way and talking about me behind their hands. Unfortunately, not being a movie star, I don't appreciate the attention. I thought you might have the same experience."

"Relax, I was just kidding. It would be nice to go out

without people coming over to say hi and interrupting my meal. I love Mexican food and the Whole Enchilada is the best."

"Great. How about Friday at six? I'll pick you up then."

After making a note of her address, Brad hung up with a smile. *See, that wasn't so bad. I'll call and make a reservation for six-thirty so we have plenty of time to get there. I feel like a teenager going to the prom, happy but scared.*

***

Friday came quickly. Brad stood in front of his closet trying to decide what to wear. *I can't remember being so nervous. I don't want to get too dressed up, but jeans might be too casual. I want her to know I like her, but not read too much into it. Khaki's, a plaid button-down shirt, and a sweater should be okay. Not too dressy and not to casual.*

Little did he know as he drove over to Christina's house, that she was dealing with the same dilemma. She had tried on several outfits before deciding on one. Pulling into the driveway, he admired the snug, little, ranch house overlooking a canyon filled with pines and scrub brush. Through the trees, he could see the ocean. When he rang the doorbell, Christina appeared in a pair of black jeans, a flowing white blouse, and a chunky turquoise necklace.

Despite the simple outfit, she looked beautiful with her shoulder-length hair hanging loosely around her face.

"Come in, come in. I like a man who is prompt. I just have to get my coat, unless you would like to have a drink first?"

"And I like a woman who doesn't keep me waiting!" They both laughed. "I'll pass on the drink; I think we should go. We can have a drink at the bar if we get there too early. Your house is really beautiful. Are those Navaho rugs?"

"Yes, I thought they would go well with the Arts and Crafts furniture I like."

"It fits just right. I have Mission Style furniture in my place and you would feel right at home there."

"I'd love to see it sometime. Right now, though, I'm ready for some Mexican food and maybe a margarita."

***

The Whole Enchilada was bustling with patrons and filled with the smell of meat, onions, chili and cumin. The mustard walls and colorful decorations added to the atmosphere.

Taking a deep breath, Christina sighed. "This was a great idea. I get hungry just walking in the door. I can never understand when people say they don't like Mexican food. I think they confuse fast food meals with the real thing. Not everything is covered in beans and cheese. I love the subtle way they add flavor here without burning your taste buds."

"Me too, I'm glad I made a reservation. This place is packed on the weekends. Do you see anything you like?"

Christina gave him a long look, that made him squirm, looked carefully at the menu and said, "A margarita for sure, and then the Crepes Sofia. It's crab season and I love the way they wrap them in crepes with the cilantro lime sauce. "

"That sounds great. I think I'll try the steak fajitas. I try to stay away from meat during the week, but weekends are red meat time! How about some guacamole and chips while we wait?"

A waiter came over bringing fresh drinks. "We didn't order these."

"Yes sir, I know. The couple at that table over there sent them over."

Christina and Brad turned to see an elderly couple at a table by the wall who waved when they looked over. "Oh, that's the Martin family. He came in last year having a heart attack and I was able to get him stabilized and connected him with a surgeon who did a bypass surgery. Let me just go over and quickly say thank you for the drinks and see how he is doing."

Brad watched her walk over and take the hands of the couple. You could see the love and gratitude in their eyes for what she had done for them. He was, once again, impressed with her caring and concern for her patients."

Christina returned shortly. "They are such a sweet couple. You know they have been married fifty years and seem to be as much in love now as newlyweds."

The evening flew by with a long discussion on local events and a little time spent trying to figure out who they knew in common. They also talked about furniture styles.

"You know, I was never too sure about the difference between Arts and Crafts, Mission and Prairie style furniture, so I recently looked it up. I always said my house was Arts and Crafts, but it's really a mix of Prairie style and Mission style. I found out the Arts and Crafts usually refers to handmade furniture while Mission is more machine made. Prairie is the Frank Lloyd Wright style with long lines and open spaces. They are all sort of lumped together in one category since they are so similar."

"Wow, that's interesting. I didn't know that. I guess my house is also Mission style. I definitely can't afford to buy all handmade furniture. People think doctors have a lot of money, but they also have a lot of debt from medical school. One time, when I was in New Jersey I went to Craftsman Farms, where Gustav Stickley made his furniture. I fell in love with the look. It was fantastic, but the house was really dark. Back in his day they only had fifteen-watt lightbulbs or candles. So, there wasn't a lot of light. I bet they all went to bed early!" Christina laughed.

Brad smiled too. "And no computers to keep them awake! I spend way too much time at work and at home, tied to my gadgets. When I finally get off them, my mind is racing with all the images and ideas."

"You wouldn't believe how many neck, hand, wrist and back problems I see because of people spending too much time on social media. That doesn't even count the mental anguish of people who have been trolled online by mean, greedy people with no concept of what havoc they are causing. People will say things online that they would never say directly to someone's face. Don't get me started." Christina growled.

"I think the staff is gently nudging us to release this table. I can't believe we have been here two hours already!"

"It was so nice to get away from work and the stress of dealing with murder and other crimes for a while. Thank you. Maybe we can do this again?"

"Christina wrapped her arm around his as they left and answered, "I would love to."

11

Brad saw Tom Kent enter the building and motioned him over. "Hi Tom, I want to ask about what you found out about the murdered woman. However, I'd like to first say how sorry I was to hear that your brother was murdered. I'm sorry I didn't talk to you immediately when you mentioned it. Do you want to talk about it?"

Tom sat on the edge of the desk. "Frank was my younger brother. He was always a fan of the Chicago Cubs, so when he was old enough to go to college, he chose Loyola university in Chicago. He was over the mountain with joy when he was accepted. He loved being in a big city like Chicago. There is so much to do and see in a city like that. In his second year there he went out to eat at a great pizza place that was famous with the students for its deep-dish pie. Two rival gangs got into a fight outside and he was killed instantly by a stray bullet that flew through the window. They knew which gangs were involved, but never figured out who pulled the trigger. He was only nineteen."

"Man, I'm so sorry to hear that. That must have been tough. I can't begin to understand how that feels. If something that senseless happened to my sister I would be devastated. That would make anyone angry, but don't let it interfere with your job."

"Don't worry, I won't. I was angry for a long time, but that has been replaced with the determination to get criminals like that off the streets. I've learned to live with the pain. It just makes me want to work even harder to solve crimes. I guess everyone has scars. Some are visible and some aren't but, after a while, they don't hurt as much. However, they are always there to remind us of what we've been through."

Brad nodded in agreement and thought about some of his own scars. Especially the one caused by someone he thought loved him. "Well, let's get back to solving this case, okay? Did you find out anything when you canvassed the area?"

"No, like we thought, it was so early that none of the business owners or homeless saw anything. However, George Edwin called to say he remembered where he had seen the hat logo. He is certain it was from the *Buccaneers Bounty* restaurant on Cannery Row."

"That's a step in the right direction. Get him in here and set him up with our sketch artist before he forgets what he saw. Then we'll take the drawing over to the restaurant to see if anyone recognizes him. Finally, something to work on."

***

"You say he was Hispanic, so we will give him brown eyes and dark hair. How does that look?"

"He had a hat on, a baseball cap with the Buccaneers Bounty logo on it. I couldn't see much of his hair. Just a little in the back when he turned around. It looked freshly cut. You know, no hair on his neck and a neat edge. No facial hair either. He looked like the kid next door."

"How about the eyes?"

"They were a little closer together, but not too close. That's it."

"How about the shape of the face? Round? Long? Square?"

"Squarer, I guess. Like that! He was a good-looking kid, even features, you know what I mean? Clean-cut and normal looking."

"I think so. Were there any scars or tattoos?"

"No, none that I saw. Like I said, he was good looking. Not handsome, but he had a straight nose, even eyes, and normal ears. They didn't stick out or were too big."

As George Edwin talked, the sketch artist continued to draw.

"That's it! That's him! I only got a quick look, but I

would swear that was him."

Thank you for your time, Mr. Edwin. I'll get copies of these drawings to our officers."

***

Tom Kent brought the printout of the artist sketch to Brad. "Here's the suspect ID that George Edwin gave us. I sent out copies to the other patrolmen so they will keep an eye out for him. Do you want me to start canvassing the waterfront to see if anyone recognizes him?"

"I think we should start at the *Buccaneers Bounty* to see if anyone there knows him. Then you can go to the other shops. You ready?"

"Sure, let's go."

12

B rad and Tom knocked on the door of the *Buccaneers Bounty* to get the attention of a man who was setting up tables for the lunch crowd.

"Go away, we're not open yet. We open at eleven."

Brad tapped his badge on the window and gestured that they should open the door.

The man walked over quickly and let them into the restaurant. "I'm so sorry, Officer. I thought you were just an early diner. My name is Frank Ciccetti. I am the owner. How can I help you?"

"I'm Detective Brad Evans with the Monterey Police Department and this is Officer Tom Kent. We were wondering if you would look at this sketch and tell us if you recognize him?"

"I think that's Eduardo Hernandez. Is he in trouble? He is a good kid. He's helped out here for years. We never had any problems with him."

"Is he here now?"

"No, but he should be here any minute to help with the set-up. He doesn't have any regular hours because he goes to Monterey Peninsula College too. We cut him some slack because he is such a good worker. There he is now. Hey Ed, these officers want to talk to you."

The young man looked in the direction of Frank, but when he saw Kent's uniform he ran back where he came from, tossing a couple of chairs down after him.

"Tom, go after him!"

Tom leapt over the fallen chairs and ran into the back. As he entered the kitchen, he ran past the gaping cooks and out the back door that was slowly closing. The backdoor led into an alley filled with empty cartons, garbage cans and debris. Right behind Tom, a number of people, in white coats and hats, poured out the door and scattering in all directions. He ignored them and continued down the alley to the street. In the distance he could see Eduardo grab a bike. Just as he was about to hop on the bike, Brad came at him from a different direction and knocked him over.

"Stay down! Hands behind your back! Why did you run? We just want to ask you some questions. Tom, read him his rights and then cuff him. I think we will do the questioning back at the station."

***

Eduardo sat in a chair by a table in the interrogation room. Brad sat kitty-corner to him while Tom stood in the back by the door. There was a camera in the corner and a red light showed it was recording everyone in the room.

"This is Detective Brad Evans, the date is November 15, 2019, one p.m. With me is Eduardo Hernandez and Officer Tom Kent. Eduardo, this conversation is being recorded. Do you understand? Do you need an interpreter?"

"No, I speak English. Why did you arrest me?"

"We have reasonable suspicion that you have information regarding a dead woman that was found on Del Monte beach. Right now, I want to know why you ran when you saw us?"

"I thought you were I.C.E., man. I thought you were here to take me away."

"Monterey does not turn people over to Immigration and Customs Enforcement. Why, are you here illegally?"

"I've lived most of my life in California. My parents brought me here when I was a baby."

"We aren't here to arrest Dreamers. We wanted to ask you about a body that was found on Del Monte Beach." Brad looked at Eduardo and noticed that he reacted to the question with surprise. Reasonable suspicion could keep him here for a short interrogation, but then he'd either have to be arrested or released. For now, Brad was happy to let him assume he was under arrest.

"I don't know what you mean. What body?"

"I think you do know what I mean. We have a credible witness who identified you as the person he saw dragging a woman out of the surf."

"I want a lawyer. You said you would provide me with a lawyer. I'm not saying anything else until you get me a lawyer."

"Okay, Tom, take him to a holding cell while we call a lawyer. Do you have a lawyer or do you want us to get a court appointed lawyer?"

"I guess you will have to appoint one."

13

It's so dark. The water is so cold. Where is Mommy? I can't see her. The waves keep splashing in my face. There she is! Mommy! Mommy, wake up! She's not moving. Man hit her so hard and threw her overboard. When he turned toward me, I jumped. Mommy taught me how to swim when he wasn't around. She said I had to know how to swim if the boat sank. He's turning the boat away from us. Where is he going? Isn't he going to help Mommy? He's leaving us all alone. Mommy, wake up! I keep shaking her, but she won't wake up. Oh no, I can't see her since that last wave. There is a light ahead. I'll swim that way. She told me, that no matter what happens, I should save myself. Maybe she is going that way too. I'm so cold. The waves keep pounding on me and the salt makes my eyes sting.

Finally, I can touch the ground. I can barely crawl up out of the water, but I'll make it. I'll save myself. Just like Mommy told me. I'll sit here for a while to see if she comes. I'm so tired.

I must have fallen asleep. I don't see Mommy anywhere. Who is that man over there with the candle? How come the candle doesn't blow out in the wind? Maybe he knows where Mommy is.

He's gesturing to me. I think he wants me to go with him. I know I am not supposed to trust anyone, but I'm not afraid of him. I can feel that he is good. He's taken my hand. His touch feels like it is barely there. He's leading me up the street and away from the beach. There is a big building ahead of us and he is opening the heavy doors. He gestures me inside and points to one of the benches. I don't know why I am here, but at least I am out of the rain. Maybe Mommy is going to meet us here. He is sitting next to me, but he hasn't said anything. He has a nice smile though. I wonder why his black dress isn't wet from the rain? Yawn, I am so tired. I'll just rest here until Mommy comes.

Claire awoke with a start. It took a minute for her to remember where she was. After a couple of days in the hospital, she was taken to this other place. Bea said it was a place that helps children who are all alone. She called it Bates. I miss Bea. First, Mommy leaves me and now the nice lady, Bea. She dabbed at the tears forming in her eyes with her nightgown as she tried to shake off the effects of the dream she had of being in the water.

I'll survive. I'll save myself.

14

Bea entered the foyer at the Bates Eldridge Family Advocacy Center. After checking in, she was led to the director's office.

"Come in, come in. You must be Bea Oakley. I heard a lot about you from the staff at CHOMP (Community Hospital of Monterey). They told me you have gotten very close to our little Jane Doe."

"I really have. Despite everything she has been through, she is a sweet little girl. I hope you don't mind that I call her Claire, I just found Jane Doe so impersonable for a small child."

"I heard you were doing that, but I wouldn't advise getting too close to her. She is very sweet, but she has experienced physical abuse and abandonment. She is traumatized and may not be able to reciprocate your feelings Right now we are looking to see if we can find any family."

"Has she said anything to you yet?"

"No, not yet. I have an Art Therapist coming in today to see if she will reveal anything in her drawings. You can watch through the window, but I don't want anything to distract her from the session."

"I've really missed her. She latched on to me after I found her in the church. I have done all the requirements to be a foster parent. Do you think Protective Services would let me foster her until her parents are located?"

"I'm not the one who makes those decisions, but I can make a recommendation. You can talk to them about it, but she needs to spend a while with us first, for evaluation."

***

Bea was watching as Claire sat at a table with her back to the window. The therapist had placed a paper and markers in front of her.

"Hello, my name is Julie. What's your name? That's alright, you don't have to talk, but I would like it if you would."

Claire continued to look down at the paper on the table. Her shoulders were hunched forward and her head was down. She glanced sideways at Julie and then quickly back at the table.

"I have a paper here and I would like you to draw a picture for me. Can you do that?"

Claire slowly reached for a black marker and thought for a moment before drawing a line horizontally across the page. She moved back and forth until everything below the line was black. Then she drew a boat on the water.

"That's very nice. Is that your boat?" Claire nodded.

"Is anyone else on the boat?" Claire added a very small figure and then used the marker to scribbled over the figure and then threw the marker across the room.

"Is that your mother? Your father? You?" Claire did not respond so the therapist took another piece of paper and said, "Can you draw me a picture of your family?"

This time, Claire looked at her and then began drawing three figures. First, she drew a small figure wearing a dress, with yellow hair, and blue eyes. Then she drew a bigger figure who also had yellow hair, blue eyes and a dress."

"Is that you and your mother? Very nice. Do you have a daddy too?"

Claire picked up another black marker and on the far edge of the page she drew another figure. It was twice the size of the mother and child. It had pants and a shirt, but the significant part was the face. She drew a jagged, open mouth and then pounded the face with her marker to cover it with dots.

Bea drew back from the window with a look of concern on her face. "I've never seen her display anger before. She has been sad or frightened, but never angry. Would it be possible to see her today? I don't want her to think I have abandoned her too."

"Not until her session with the art therapist is over. A short visit would be alright, but I have to warn you again to not get too attached to her."

***

As Claire exited the therapy room, she saw Bea and ran to her and grabbed her around the legs.

"Oh, sweet Claire, how are you? I missed you so much. I can only stay for a little bit, but I wanted to bring you a little present."

Bea pulled a small Raggedy Ann doll out of her purse. "This is for you. See, if you look under her blouse, there is a little heart."

Claire took the doll and looked at the heart, then she hugged it to her chest and cradled it like a baby. She turned to Bea with a bright smile. "Thank you," she whispered.

The adults beamed at each other but did not make a fuss that she had finally, spoken a couple of words. However, Bea reached down and gave her a bear hug. "When I can't be here with you, you can look at the doll and know that you are in my heart. I'll be back again soon."

15

Tom Kent entered the room and walked over to Brad Evans desk. 'Brad, I just picked up the DNA results from our victim. You were right, the child and the woman are directly related."

"Did they have the DNA from the father?"

"Yes, there was a link from the child and I checked it through the database. You won't want to hear who it is."

Brad grabbed the report and flipped through it quickly. He stopped on the page with the father's DNA results. "Okay, I'll bite, who is the father?"

Tom handed him another sheet of paper. On it was a mug shot and statistics of previous crimes. "His name is Eliott James. He has a rap sheet as long as my arm. Sexual assault, assault and battery, drugs and just about anything else you can think of. He has been in and out of jail since he was a kid. I called the police at the last place he was arrested. After being released from jail he skipped his parole meetings and left town. No one has seen him since."

Looking over the sheet, Brad said, "He is an ugly son of a gun. Look at all those pock marks on his face. I wonder how he ever ended up with a girl as pretty as our Jane Doe? Maybe it was a one-night stand and not a relationship. Looking at this sheet, he may have raped her and got her pregnant. At any rate, we need to find this guy and hear his story. If he is the father of the little girl then he has some explaining to do. Either he has been abusing her or someone else did. I wouldn't be surprised if he is the one who caused the head injury on our Jane Doe. With his background it wouldn't be a stretch of the imagination for him to move from assault to murder."

"I also did some checking on our Jane Doe. There was a girl in Oregon listed as missing, about eight years ago, that looks a lot like our woman. The DNA matches. Her name was Stephanie Goodwin. She ran away from a group home where she was living and just disappeared. There are no living relatives. Her disappearance coincides with James falling off the grid."

"No living relatives, except for the little girl."

"Sure, except for her. What a tough life to have a dead mother and a deadbeat father like James."

"Let's talk to Eduardo again and see if he can fill in any of the gaps. His lawyer, Sam Johnson, got him out of here. Can you give him a call and have him bring Eduardo back?"

***

Brad entered the room where Eduardo Hernandez and his lawyer were sitting. "Hey, Sam, it's good to see you again. How's the wife and kids?"

"They're great. The little one just turned three and is cute as a button. I'm glad to see you back at work after what happened last year."

"Thanks. I had a good doctor and Bea wouldn't let me do anything until I was well again."

"Good for her. Knowing you, you'd be out swimming laps a week after getting stabbed. Let's get down to business. My client was an innocent bystander in the death of the woman on the beach. I read your report and there is no indication he did anything wrong. He pulled her from the water, thinking he could help her somehow."

"Well, he did run away from us when all we wanted to do was talk to him."

"He was afraid you were going to turn him over to the I.C.E. agents."

"You know we don't do that here."

"Sure, I know it, but he didn't. From the report it is clear that his footprints came from the bike path. When he arrived at work, he was not wet like he had been swimming in the bay. There is no evidence that he was anything but a good citizen trying to help someone in need,"

"Again, why did he run when George Edwin asked him if he needed help?"

Sam looked at Eduardo and nodded that he should answer the question.

"When I pulled her up onto the beach, I could tell she was dead. When that guy yelled at me, I ran because I knew it wouldn't look good. Everyone thinks that Hispanics are all bad, but I was just trying to help! I'm undocumented, so I learned early, to keep my head down and to stay out of trouble. Ask my boss. He'll tell you I wouldn't do anything bad."

"Actually, when I talked to him, he said you were a good kid who was honest and trustworthy. There doesn't seem to be anything linking you to her death. We'd like to know though, if you saw anything, anything at all, that might help us find the killer? Did you see anyone else around? Did you take anything from where you found her? Did you hear or see anything unusual?"

"She was killed? I thought she drowned. No. I didn't see anyone until Mr. Edwin showed up. Not too many people go walking on the beach that early on a rainy day. It's hard to hear anything over the sound of the waves and harbor seals. I saw her in the water and pulled her out. Then I ran. I didn't see anything or take anything. Until that man yelled at me all I heard were the waves lapping on the shore and the sea lions barking."

"If you think of anything else, here's my card. Please call. You are free to go, but don't leave town."

"Sam, thanks for coming in. Please make sure your client doesn't disappear. If he hadn't ran the first time, he would have just been asked some questions and let go. You might want to help him get his citizenship papers so he doesn't have to live in fear all the time. He seems like a good kid and a benefit to our town."

"I don't do that kind of work, but I know someone who can probably help. I'll do what I can, but the country is divided on how to treat Dreamers. Luckily, California knows we need and want good people, wherever they come from or however they got here. Since Dreamers were brought here by their parents, they didn't have much of a say so, and many people feel they should be given a chance to become citizens. Can you do anything to keep his name off the books? It's hard enough to get citizenship without a police record."

"I'll see that he is just listed as a witness. Maybe next time, he will not be as afraid of us."

"Thank you so much Detective, I will make sure that I don't disappoint you. It would be so fantastic to be legal for the first time in my life." Eduardo pumped Brad's hand energetically and left, smiling, with his lawyer.

16

B rad and Christina were walking on the pedestrian path near Lovers Point in Pacific Grove. The weather was warm with a slight breeze coming off the water and blowing her hair. She reached up and smoothed it back. Brad was watching her, thinking about how her hair looked like golden silk.

"Look, there's a Monarch butterfly! It's so amazing that they find their way to this little town on the way to Mexico. They are usually here in abundance in October and November, but a couple of strays can be seen at other times too. I remember having a field trip to the Butterfly Park when I was in school. The guide told us that so many congregate on the trees in that little grove that their weight can actually break a branch on the eucalyptus trees."

Christina looked at Brad in amazement. "I didn't know that. I grew up in the Central Valley so we didn't learn about them like you did. They are really beautiful with their orange and black wings."

"Have you ever been to the butterfly parade? The school kids and even some pets, put on butterfly wings and parade through town. It is so cute to see those first and second graders with their wings askew. In many ways, Pacific Grove really is 'Americas Last Home Town'. They try to keep the old traditions, but progress is slowly overtaking them."

"I know, I've read about the fight between the locals and the people who use their houses for short-term rentals. With a revolving door of people coming and going, it's hard to keep the feeling of neighborhood and community."

"Speaking of traditions, what are you doing on Thanksgiving? Are you going home? Are you working? Bea always hosts the meal and everyone brings a dish. It's an open door and most of us bring a friend or two. I thought I'd ask Tom Kent, the officer who replaced Jimmy Williams, and you, if you want."

"I would love that! My parents have passed away and I am an only child, so there isn't a "home" to go back to now. Luckily, I also have that day off. What can I bring? I make a mean apple pie."

"That sounds great. I'll tell Bea."

"I know this is probably rude, but can I bring one of the other doctors with me? She is new to the area and I know she is going to be alone that day."

"I'm sure Bea won't mind. You've met her. The only thing bigger than her table is her heart."

***

"Pat, get the door! I think our guests are starting to arrive!"

Pat Oakley went to the door of their Spanish style bungalow. It was only about a thousand feet square, but once inside, it felt roomy and inviting.

"Hi Brad, oh, and Doctor Velk. Welcome, welcome. Come in. Here, let me take that from you. This pie smells delicious. Is it pumpkin? Yum. You can hang your jackets on the pegs near the door. Who is this lovely young lady?"

"Pat, you know Christina, and this is her friend from work, Doctor Susan Blake. Remember, I told you they were coming."

"Of course. The more the merrier. Especially ones who come bearing food. What do we have here, doctor?"

"Please call me Sue. Thank you so much for allowing me to join you. I'm new here and it was either be alone on Thanksgiving or offer to work. This is a much better choice. I thought I would go traditional and bring a green bean casserole."

Bea entered just as the introductions were taking place. "Oh yum, I hope it's one of those with the fried onion rings. Thanksgiving is the one time of the year that I let Pat lets me pig out. The rest of the time I keep him on a healthy diet, heavy on vegetables. He is going to love this!"

"Well, as a doctor I have to agree with Bea. But, everything in moderation. Eating comfort food once in a while won't hurt."

Bea wiped her hands on an apron that said, "Kiss the Cook". Putting an arm around Pat she said, "I just want to keep him around as long as possible. I doubt if I could find another man as wonderful as he is!"

Blushing, Pat took the pie into the kitchen while Bea invited the guests into the living room. "What can I get everyone to drink? We have cranberry juice, beer, wine or sodas. Brad, please pour the drinks while I take the green beans into the kitchen."

When Brad returned with the drinks, Bea was back and in deep conversation with the two women. "So, Sue, where did you move here from?"

"I used to live in New Jersey, but I wanted to get out and see something beside the Garden State. I went to school at Stanford, and when I heard there was an opening at CHOMP for an ER doctor, I applied. I just moved here last month."

"Where did you live in New Jersey? I have some very close friends who live outside of Morristown."

"I was farther south, outside of Trenton."

Christina said, "People always say that New Jersey isn't nice, but when I visited my friends, I was pleasantly surprised. The forests and hills, lakes and shore line are beautiful. The quaint towns and history are amazing. Of course, I am partial to this area where we don't have to shovel snow in the winter or have humidity in the summer. People here say we live in Paradise."

"I've only been here a short while, but I have to admit it is beautiful. Deep down though, I guess I'll always be a "Jersey Girl".

Bea and Pat's sons, Patty and Wally, came in from the backyard with another two people.

"I'd like you to meet our sons. This is Pat Junior; we call him Patty. He is a Senior at UCLA and this is his girlfriend, June Howe. And this is our other son, Wally. He is a Junior at Berkley. He brought a friend too."

"This is my friend, Jerrod Johnson. We room together."

"Boys, you know Doctor Velk and this is her friend, Doctor Susan Blake."

"I think you are all old enough to call us Christina and Sue. Right Sue?"

"Sure, I'm not that much older than you all. It would feel weird for you to call me doctor all the time."

Bea excused herself and went to check on the dinner.

The women offered to help but she said that the kitchen was small and she and Pat had a routine working together.

"I will accept your help though, with the clean-up after dinner. By then I will be dead on my feet. Why don't you all go into the back room to watch the football game."

Brad went to the door to let another guest in. "Welcome Tom! I'm glad you could come. Can I get you a drink?"

"Sure, a beer sounds good. Thanks for inviting me. I brought a plate of hot wings and veggies. I wasn't sure what you needed and I'm not much of a cook."

"That's perfect. Why don't you take them into the back room while I get your beer. The guys are watching the football game. I'll be right there."

Tom took his plate of snacks into the room where he heard alternating yells and sighs as the game pivoted from one teams' advantage to the other."

"Come on in. We welcome anyone bearing food!" Patty introduced Tom around the group and invited him to take a seat.

"You must be Tom, Brad's new right-hand man."

"Well, I wouldn't say that, but we are working a couple of cases together."

By the time Brad appeared with his beer, Tom was ensconced on the couch next to Sue.

"Who's ahead?"

"Who cares? We just picked a side to root for. Since our schools aren't playing, none of us is invested in the game. It's always more interesting when we have a connection somehow to a team. This time, none of us does." A roar went up from the opposite side of the room when their *pretend* favorites scored a touchdown.

Bea came in to ask how long until the game was over. Brad answered, "Anytime the food is ready, so are we. We can watch football anytime, but we don't get food like this very often."

"Alright then, let's eat!"

***

The dinner was filled with laughter and friendly chatter as family and friends filled themselves with food and the warm hospitality of their hosts. Bea had set the table with her fine china and crystal glassware. It looked like a Norman Rockwell painting with a huge turkey in the middle of the table, beans, mashed potatoes, brussels sprouts, glazed carrots, beets, stuffing, gravy, rolls and cranberries, surrounding the Fall flowers that decorated the white tablecloth.

"Bea, you have outdone yourself. The table is beautiful and everything smells delicious."

"Thanks, Christina, I couldn't have done it without all your help. I love having my house and table full. It's too quiet with just Pat and me around."

"Remember the time Wally wanted to be a circus acrobat and ended up breaking his leg when he tried to walk a rope from the tree and the house?!"

"I sure do. Not only did he break a leg, he broke the tree in half."

"Ha, ha, very funny. What about the time you tried to do a flip with your bicycle and ended up with a concussion, Patty?!"

"I hear there is a lot of snow up in the mountains this year. Anyone planning on going skiing?"

"I'd sure like to, but my classes are keeping me really busy. I barely have time to breathe." Patty sighed.

"I can vouch for that! He spends more time talking about his Senior Seminar than he does about us!" June looked at him with a smile that softened her critical words.

"You should talk! The last time I took you to a movie, you fell asleep. Senior year has been tough on both of us."

Bea lifted her glass, "Let's drink to our hardworking students! At least you are taking it seriously and not spending your time sowing wild oats." Bea looked over her glass at Brad.

"Hey, I turned out alright. I even graduated with

honors. Speaking of students, have you decided on a major yet, Wally?"

"Well, I was going to talk to you later, but I was thinking of going into law. Specifically, law enforcement."

"That's great. You'd make a wonderful police officer. I'd suggest finishing your undergraduate classes and then decide if you want to go for a law degree or into the police academy. Either way, you are adding more years of study. Lawyers make more money, but...maybe I'm biased... I doubt they get the same feeling of satisfaction I do when I solve a case."

"I'll keep that in mind, but I really admire the good you do. Why did you join the police force, Brad?"

"I was always really good at puzzles and I liked helping people. When I have a case to solve, it is like doing a big, complicated puzzle. You have to sort all the pieces and see where they all fit together."

Christina added, "Being a doctor is sort of like that too. I sift through the symptoms and tests and come up with likely causes for the illness. Of course, sometimes it's obvious, like when Brad came into the ER with a stab wound. Other times, it is difficult, like when he was poisoned. There could be multiple causes for the symptoms he had."

Bea said, "We are so grateful for what you did for him. The peace of mind you give your patients and families must make you feel good too. Do you have some kind of magic spell that would keep him out of your ER for a while?"

"I wish I did. It makes me feel good to help other people, but I wasn't fishing for compliments. Being a doctor is a challenge and a pleasure."

Pushing back from the table, Brad said, "I don't think I can eat another bite. Everything was delicious. Here's to Bea and Pat and the many cooks who contributed to the feast."

Everyone raised their glasses in a toast. Christina added, "It was so kind of you all to invite an orphan like me to your family meal. It's been the best Thanksgiving I've had in a long time."

"Speaking of orphans, there is something I want to run by all of you. You know about the little girl I found in the church a couple of weeks ago. Pat and I have been talking, and we would like to be foster parents to her until her case is resolved. I would like to know what you think."

"Where would she sleep?"

"I thought you and Wally could sleep in the same room. You aren't home that much anymore, Patty, and soon, you will be off on your own. I hope you don't mind."

"That's fine with me, if Wally is okay with it."

"Sure. I can move my stuff into Patty's room. It's bigger than mine."

Brad spoke, "I think it's great you want to do this, Bea. I know you have formed a bond with her and you already have your foster parent certification. Are you sure you can help a child who doesn't even speak? It's a big responsibility."

"I agree with Brad. It is very nice of you to want to help her, but as a doctor, I have to ask if you have thought through all the problems of a child who has been through what she has experienced?"

"We have. I know it won't be easy, but if we can't help a child who is so in need of love, who should we help? She has been improving lately. Her weight is back in the normal range and she actually said a couple of words the other day when I brought her a gift. We definitely have a bond. She has even been warming up to Pat when we have gone to see her together. We aren't even sure if they will allow us to have her. Are there any other thoughts?"

Everyone looked at each other to see if they wanted to say anything, but no one had anything to add.

"Okay then, lets raise our glasses and toast to giving that child a home!"

17

The Oakley house was in chaos. Wally was moving his things into Patty's room and Bea and Pat were setting up a new bed in Patty's room. Boxes were being sorted as trash, move, or store in the garage. There was some good-natured squabbling among the boys about territory and boundaries, while Bea and Pat were laying a tarp to paint Wally's old room.

"Let's leave the glow-in-the-dark stars on the ceiling, but we really need to paint the walls where Wally took down all his old posters. I bought a light grey paint for the walls. It should go well with the seaside designed sheets and comforter for her bed. I also bought a couple of outfits for her to wear. You never know what she will come with from Protective Services. Once she settles in, we can look for anything else she needs."

"Now Bea, remember that she is just a foster child. She may be with us a long time or just a few weeks. If they find her family, we will have to give her up. You can't let yourself get too attached."

"I know, I know, but it's already too late to not get attached. I feel like a mama bear every time I see her. I'll do anything to protect her and try to put a smile on that cute face."

"The doctor's report says she is about seven years old, but small for her age. Probably caused by lack of protein and nutrition as she was growing. They suggested I keep her in therapy for a while to help her work through the trauma that she has experienced. The art therapist says her drawings show a definite separation between her and her father. Whether the separation is physical or emotional, it is hard to say until she starts to talk more. Brad told me that the DNA test showed her father to be an ex-con with a violent streak. That would certainly explain the bruising and broken bones. I just want to make her life a little better."

"I understand, Bea, but we aren't that young anymore. Raising a child can be hard at times, but we could handle it when we were young. Now, to take on this girl, with all her problems, do you think we can do it?"

"Oh, Pat. We aren't twenty anymore, but we aren't old either. I know lots of couples who have children in their forties. I thought we both agreed we would do this."

"We did. Maybe I'm just nervous. It's been a long time since the boys were small. I'm afraid that most of the work is going to fall on your shoulders."

"I want to do this. We can do this. If her father is the monster, we think he is, then you can be a big help in getting her to trust men. You can show her the love and respect that a real man gives women and children. There, the painting is done. After it dries, we can move the bed back against the wall. I'm excited...you know I always wanted a little girl. She may not be mine, but I can spoil her while she is here."

Bea placed a doll that she had as a girl on the bed and went to check on the boys.

As she entered the room, she could see their red curly hair bent over as they looked at some of the comic books Wally found when he was clearing out his room.

"Mom, look at what Wally found! It's his old collection of Marvel comic books. They are in great condition. I wonder if they are worth anything on eBay?"

"Hey wait a minute, you're not going to sell my comic books. I still want them."

"Guys, I am so glad you are okay with me bringing Claire into our home. I am proud of both of you. When you come home for Christmas break, I hope you will get to know her like I do. She is a sweet little thing, but has already been through a lot in her life."

"I know Mom. We realize how lucky we have been to grow up in a loving family. We never wanted for anything. You were always there for us. Right Wally?"

"Yes, I know we don't tell you, but we are lucky to

have you and Dad as parents. Now that I am away at college, I realize that a lot of kids didn't have the love we had. We never had to worry about where our next meal would come from or if our parents didn't love us. You always supported us…and still do."

"I couldn't be prouder of you both. If we can help this child, we will be doing one of the best things a person can do. The Jewish faith has a saying, "Save a life, Save the world." During the Holocaust, it was especially true for the ones who were able to save some Jewish people from death. In Claire's case, if we can help her, we are saving her future, her world."

18

A small, white, car with an official looking Monterey County sticker on the side, pulled into the driveway of the Oakley home. Through the window, a small girl could be seen clutching a Raggedy Ann doll and looking apprehensively toward the house.

Bea and Pat ran onto the driveway before they had put the car in park. "There you are! We have been waiting for you."

"Bea jumped to the window every time she heard a car go by. I'm Pat Oakley, the silent half of the Oakley family." He reached out his hand to the woman who was stepping out of the driver's seat.

Bea, jabbed him in the ribs as he turned around. "You may be my other half, but you are definitely not silent!"

Smiling, the woman greeted them. "Hello, Bea, it's good to see you again. Let's get this little lady out of the car and into her new home."

As they walked around the car, Claire was tugging at the door, trying to get out. "Wait just a minute until I unlock the door!"

The woman pushed her key fob and Claire jumped from the car. She ran directly to Bea and put an arm around her waist. The other arm clung tightly to her doll, which was decidedly more worn since Bea had given it to her.

"Hello sweet girl. Do you remember my husband, Pat? He visited you in the hospital. While you are staying with us, I hope you will become good friends. Come in, Come in. There's no reason for us to be standing out here."

Pat grabbed the plastic garbage bag, with Claire's belongings and followed them into the house.

"Would you like to see the room you will be staying in? Please, Mrs. West, come too. I want you to see where her room is."

As they entered the bedroom, Claire just stood in the doorway looking at everything. "Go ahead, darling. This is going to be your room. It used to be my son, Wally's, room. He is away at college right now, but both of my boys will be home for Christmas. He is going to be sleeping in his brother, Patty's, room, so this room is all for you. Do you like it?"

Claire hugged her doll tighter to her chest and walked slowly into the room. She sat on the edge of the bed and bounced up and down a little. She looked at the doll on the bed and put her Raggedy Ann doll next to it. She touched the other dolls eyes, which moved up and down. Pat came in with the bag of her things and started to hang her clothes in the closet. Claire watched him and then went over and peaked in the closet. She looked at the other clothes hanging there and touched a couple of dresses tenderly. She glanced back at Bea as if asking if these were really hers.

"Yes, honey, those are for you. We can go shopping after you have settled in and get anything else you may need. You can put your underwear and socks in the dresser over there."

After she put away her things, Claire walked over to the window and looked out at the neat front yard. Pat worked for the Parks department and believed in drought resistant plants to survive the frequent dry periods in California. His yard was filled with succulents and cacti. There wasn't any lawn because he felt it was a waste of precious water. One lemon tree with bare, winter, branches was in the corner near the neighbor's lot and a palm tree was on the other side of the yard. It was a quiet street with very little traffic.

"Why don't I show you where the bathroom is? It is a small house so you will have to share it with the boys when they are home, but most of the time it will be all yours." Bea placed Claire's hairbrush in the bathroom cabinet and her toothbrush near the sink. "Do you need to use the bathroom?"

Claire shook her head so they continued on their tour of the house. "Our bedroom is across from yours and the boys are on the other side of the bathroom. You saw the dining room when you came in and here in the back of the house is the family room with the television and computer. Now let me show you the kitchen." Bea led them into the bright kitchen. There were modern, maple, cabinets with stainless appliances and refrigerator. A big window above the sink and one near the dining room let in bright sunlight. Claire ran to the window when she saw a hummingbird fly over to one of the bird feeders hanging from a pergola in the backyard.

"That's a hummingbird. He is very territorial and chases all the other birds away from the feeder. I tried other bird feeders, but the squirrels ate all the food. So now we have just the one feeder and the one hummingbird that calls us home. Sometimes you can hear an owl in the neighbor's trees or pigeons on the roof. Of course, there are crows too. If you like birds we can take you out to Elkhorn Slough to see all the egrets and other water fowl. Pat, would you take Claire out to the backyard while I have a little chat with Mrs. West?"

"I'd love to. Claire, do you want to go out and try the new swing set we bought?" Gently taking her hand, he led her into the yard. She looked back at Bea, who waved her hands, making a shooing motion, to encourage Claire to go ahead.

"Now, Mrs. West, is there anything I need to know?"

"The police have told us that the dead woman on the shore is a DNA match to the girl. Our psychiatrist told her gently, but it was not as big a shock to her as I thought. I think she knew already that her mother was gone. She was very sad anyway, so that may come up in your interactions with her. We believe that she is suffering from selective mutism."

"What's that?"

"It is rare, but for some children it starts early. It's not that they don't want to talk, they are unable to talk. When someone expects them to talk, the pressure triggers a panic response, and they literally can't talk. We believe that Claire's case is caused by her abuse."

"But she said 'Thank You' to me when I gave her the doll."

"That's also typical of selective mutism. They can talk to people they trust, but freeze around strangers. I think your relationship with her will encourage her to talk more and more and, hopefully, realize that she need not be afraid of others. Of course, she should continue with therapy as well."

"Oh, that is good news. I have a friend who is a child therapist. Can she go to her or do I have to continue with your psychiatrist?"

"That is fine. She just has to file reports with us so we can follow her progress. Your house is lovely and it looks like you are ready to take on this responsibility. If you need any advice, please call me. Here is my card. I will be doing visits occasionally to check up on things, but don't be nervous. I'm sure you will be fine."

"Would you like to say goodbye to her before you go?"

Bea led Mrs. West out to the backyard where Pat was pushing a smiling child on the swings. Claire would lean her head back so that she was almost flat and her hair would sway in the wind. They watched for a couple of minutes until the swing came to rest and Claire ran over to Bea and grabbed her hand. Bea bent down, "Claire, Mrs. West is going to leave now. You are going to stay here with Pat and me."

Claire looked shyly at the woman and then held out her hand to shake. "Of course, I will shake hands with you. May I give you a little hug? Good. I know you will be very happy with Bea and Pat and I will stop in once in a while, to visit."

She walked with Bea to the front of the house and got in her car. "She is a sweet little girl who has been through a lot. I know she will find peace and care here. See you soon!"

19

Brad looked around his desk at the Monterey Police Department as if the piles of paper would give him inspiration. He lifted the edge of one stack and rifled through without withdrawing anything. On the intercom he asked Tom Kent to come to his desk.

"Hi Brad, I wanted to thank you again for inviting me to Thanksgiving dinner. Your family is great. It was so nice of Bea and Pat to include me. Holidays are always a little hard since my brother was killed."

"No problem. We enjoyed having you, although, once you met Sue, she seemed to occupy all your attention."

"I'm sorry if I neglected the rest of you, but I felt like I had known her forever. She is really easy to talk to. I'm taking her out again next weekend. So, what did you want to see me about?"

"Have you found any more information on Eliott James? I seem to have hit a wall since we got the DNA tests back. Bea loves having the little girl with her, but it's only fair we try to find her father and figure out if he was involved in her mother's death."

"I've passed around his mug shot to the other officers,

but so far, there haven't been any hits. It was an old picture and he has been off the radar for many years. He may have changed a lot since then. He may also not be in the area anymore, or never was here."

"He may have changed his looks, but it would be hard to hide the pock marks on his face. We'll just have to hope that something breaks soon. Otherwise, this may end up as a cold case."

***

Bea, Pat and Claire were walking on Pacific Street in Monterey. They were following the luminaries that marked the Christmas in the Adobes path. "Claire, be sure to not get too close to the lights. We don't want the candles inside to burn the bags. Isn't it pretty? All the adobes are open to the public tonight. It only happens once a year since some of them are privately owned now. Why don't we go in this one? The House of the Four Winds always has a beautiful Christmas tree. The locals gave the house that name because of the weather vane on its roof. Mrs. Santa Claus is in the old adobe part of the building. Did you bring your wish list to give her? She'll make sure that Santa and his elves get it."

"Oh look! I forgot about their doll collection. Aren't they interesting? They were donated by one of the members of the Monterey Civic Club who had been collecting dolls for years. Some of these are very old. This old adobe from Thomas Larkin was saved from decay and is kept up by that club too. It's like stepping back in time to see these old rooms and the women in period dress. There's Mrs. Claus, go over and give her your list."

Claire walked over to the kindly woman in a red skirt, white apron, and little white mob cap. She looked over her glasses at Claire as she approached.

"Come here sweetheart. I see you have a list for Santa. What is your name?"

"I'm sorry Mrs. Claus, Claire doesn't like to speak. However, she wrote down what she wanted for Christmas."

"Well, Claire is it? You don't have to talk. So, let me look at this list. Crayons, paper, scissors, and a notebook. That's all? I'm sure Santa will be able to arrange to get these things for you. Don't you think so, Mom? Well, my elf here will give you a candy cane and then I have to talk to the other boys and girls. Merry Christmas dear."

A young boy, dressed like an elf, gave her a candy cane and Claire scurried over to Bea and Pat who were looking at the Christmas tree in the adobe.

"Aren't these ornaments beautiful? The Embroiderers Guild makes the ornaments and decorates the tree every year. I can show you how to do that too, Claire.

My grandmother taught me when I was just a little girl. Unfortunately, I have trouble now seeing the tiny stitches without a magnifying glass."

Taking a homemade cookie off the tray, they admired the Flamenco dancers in the meeting hall of the club. When the dancers stopped for a rest they moved down the road, stopping in the open adobes along the way. Some of the adobes had musicians, or people dressed in costumes from the Mexican era. Many people were walking along with Santa hats or blinking lights around their necks. The night air was warm and everything and everyone were in a festive mood.

Pat grabbed his stomach like he had to hold it up with both hands. I don't think I'll eat another cookie, ever. They are all so tasty. Let's go over to Peets for a cup of coffee and a hot chocolate for Claire." Claire smiled brightly at the mention of hot chocolate and took hold of Pat's hand.

As Pat went to the counter and ordered their drinks while Bea and Claire sat at a table. Pat didn't notice the man at one of the tables watching them closely. As they turned to leave, he raised his newspaper so they couldn't see his face. He leaned over to the woman at the next table and said, "Excuse me. Are you from around here?" She nodded as he continued. "I thought I saw an old classmate of mine. Did you see that couple with the little girl? Was that Mildred Ferguson?"

"No, you must be mistaken. That is Bea Oakley and her husband Pat. The little girl is their foster child. Sweet little thing, but she hasn't talked at all since they took her in. I hear though, that she is starting to say a word or two."

"Thanks, I guess I was wrong."

20

Eliott James paced back and forth. Occasionally he kicked at a low stone wall outside the coffee shop. *I can't believe that bratty kid is still alive. How did she survive jumping into the bay? At least it sounds like she isn't telling any tales about what happened. I'll have to get the address of that Bea Oakley and grab the kid.*

James opened his phone and started to google "Oakly." Nothing happened so he tried various spellings of the name until Patrick Oakley showed up. They lived just outside of the center of Monterey. He phoned the number listed and got the answering machine. "Hello this is the Oakley home. Bea and I are out right now, but leave your number and we will call you right back." James hung up quickly.

Well, that solves that problem. I have the address and I can hang out there until I can grab the kid. She looked happy today. I'll wipe that smile off her face. Little does she know that she will soon be joining her mother in the hereafter.

***

Bea, Pat and Claire were at their last stop of the night. San Carlos Cathedral was lit up and music from the children's choir was wafting through the air. It sounded beautiful to hear it in the air outside the illuminated church. After grabbing another cookie and some Mexican hot chocolate, they wandered over to the grotto where there was a life-sized nativity scene behind a gate.

"I'm glad they finally found all the pieces to this Nativity so they could set it up once again. The plaque here says it was donated by the Monterey Civic Club. They sure do a lot of good in Monterey. With the gate there, they don't have to worry about someone taking the baby Jesus, like so many other places have experienced. I know it is just a prank, but it really ruins things for other people who enjoy seeing the scene. See, Claire, that is the bed for the baby Jesus. His parents are called Mary and Joseph. God was the real daddy of Jesus, but Joseph was his adopted father. Sort of like Pat and I aren't your real parents, but we love and care for you too."

21

Eliott James stood behind a tree across the road from the Oakley home. *There they are. So oblivious to the danger that is all around them. Most people are so smug in their illusion of safety. Well, they'll learn soon enough that not everything is candles and Christmas carols. No one ever brought me any gifts at Christmas or even on my birthday. I was lucky if my gifts weren't a punch and a kick. Then my parents would have me kneel and beg for forgiveness. Most of the time I didn't even know what I did wrong. It was hard life, but it made me tough. These people have no clue how tough life can be.*

There, they are going to bed. It looks like the kid's bedroom is in the front. Just that much easier to get at her. All the lights are off now. I'll give them a couple more minutes and then sneak up and snatch her.

Darn! The guy is out in front just sitting in one of the chairs. What is he doing? Great, look at those huge binoculars! He is a star gazer. Just my luck that it is a clear night with a full moon. Well, no telling how long he'll be out there. I'm getting cold. Now that I know where they live, I'll come back when it's cloudy. Let's just hope she doesn't start talking before that time.

***

Claire hopped out of Bea's car and ran toward the front door. She had just been to the Del Monte Shopping Center and couldn't wait to wrap the gifts they had picked out for Pat and Brad. She turned around while she waited for Bea to catch up and open the door.

Wait, what's that in the bushes across the street? I thought it was a man. I don't see anything now. Maybe it was just a shadow. It is kind of late in the day. Everything looks different now. The setting sun makes all the shadows longer. I could have sworn I saw someone watching us.

Bea opened the door and Claire ran inside and knelt on a chair by the front window. She parted the curtains a little and stared across the street.

"Claire, what are you looking at? Did you see something? Is it a bird?" Bea looked out too, but didn't see anything out of order. "I don't see anything. Come on and let's get these presents put away before Pat gets home. We don't want to spoil his surprise."

Claire pointed to the window and said, "Man."

Bea looked again. "I don't see anyone out there now. Maybe it was just a shadow. Let's put these away and then you can help me get dinner ready. What do you think about meatloaf, green beans, and mashed potatoes?" Bea knew that, if anything could distract this little girl, it was food. She still ate like she would never eat again, sometimes to the point where here stomach hurt. *Who can blame her? Considering the condition, she was in when we found her, it doesn't look like she had a lot to eat.* Bea gazed at her, with an ache in her throat, as Claire ran to her room to hide the presents. Bea wondered if Claire would ever overcome the trauma she endured.

Eliott James ducked down behind some bushes when he saw Claire looking in his direction. *Lesson learned, don't come before dark. I was sure the brat saw me, but I guess I hid in time. I'll be back tonight when the neighborhood is quiet.*

***

Eliott James parked his car at the end of the block and walked down the street, as if he were a neighbor just out for a late-night stroll. Anyone who would look outside would just see a tall man in a baseball cap strolling along the sidewalk. His senses were alert to even the slightest sound or movement in the area. Seeing nothing amiss, he darted across the street and stopped behind a large lemon tree on the edge of the Oakley property. Checking the area again, he slowly moved toward the front bedroom window, remembering to stay in the shadows as much as possible. *Good, the window is open a crack. I'll just have to remove the screen and I will be in her room before she knows it.*

***

Claire woke to a slight sound by her window. As she looked in that direction, she saw her father at the window, removing the screen. She jumped from her bed and ran to the room next door, where Bea and Pat were deeply asleep. She didn't stop to knock on the door, but flung it open with all the strength of her little seven-year-old body. Bea and Pat both woke up with a start. Running up to their bed Claire grabbed Bea and began pulling her toward her room.

"What is it? What's wrong? Did you have a nightmare?" Reaching out to hug Claire, Bea could feel her whole-body trembling. "Now, now, It's okay. You are with us now." Claire continued to pull at her and try to draw her back toward the door. "What is it? You want me to go with you? Alright, let's go see what's the matter. Go back to sleep, Pat. I'll take care of her."

Entering the room, Bea turned on the lights and looked around. "See, there isn't anything to be afraid of. You must have been dreaming."

Claire tiptoed into the room, staying behind Bea. She pointed toward the window. "Man," She said.

Bea looked out the window and closed the window and curtain. "See nothing there either. Why don't you hop into bed and I will stay with you for a while?" Claire shook her head and wouldn't get into the bed. "You can come snuggle with us until you calm down, but then you have to go back to your own bed. I'm sure you are just imagining things. You are safe with us."

Bea pulled Claire into her bed and wrapped the child in her arms until she could feel her relax and her heartbeat start to slow down. Bea carefully carried Claire back to her room and tucked her into bed. The next thing she knew was the sun shining through the window and Claire was lifting her eyelid. "What!? Oh, Claire, that is not a nice way to wake someone. What time is it? I guess we ought to get up and get this day started. Hurry into your room and get dressed. I'll have breakfast ready as soon as I wash up."

Claire clung to Bea's pajamas and wouldn't let go. She had to pry her fingers off her pants so that she could move toward the hall. Claire followed so closely behind that Bea could hardly move. She noticed that Claire's blanket and pillow were beneath the bed. *I wonder if she slept there last night after I brought her back to her own bed?*

"I know you had a bad dream last night, but everything is fine now. See, no one in your room." As Bea drew back the curtains, she noticed the screen laying on the ground. "See, Claire, the screen fell out last night and that must be what scared you. I'll have Pat fix it today."

22

"Hi Christina, It's Brad. Oh, I guess you knew that already from the number on your screen. I, uh, I was wondering if you would like to go with me to the Lighted Boat Parade on Sunday? The Monterey Yacht Club does the parade every year. The boat owners go all out decorating their vessels with lights. Some play Christmas music and they have a fun time on board with their guests. I have a friend, Keith Waldron, who offered to take us out onto the water in his boat to watch the parade go by. Keith is a professor at Cal State University Monterey Bay. I think you'll like him. He knows a lot about the local history, and California."

"Give me a chance to answer you! Yes, I'd love to go. It sounds like a lot of fun."

"Tom and Sue are going to be there too, so you will know some people. I was surprised how they have hit it off. He can be a little intense at times. I think Sue has been good for him. I see him smiling more than he used to and they are together all the time. I'm glad you brought her along on Thanksgiving. They make a good couple."

"I think so too. Sue has been even more happy than

she usually is since they met. It will be fun to be with them."

"I'll pick you up around four-thirty. That will give us a chance to find a parking spot and help Keith get the boat ready to sail out. Don't worry about the sailing part. You don't need to know how to sail, we can do all the work. You can just sit back with a drink and enjoy the view. Be sure to dress warm. It can get really cold out on the water. Wear tennis shoes with plain soles. If you mark up the deck, Keith will make you scrub it down afterwards! Okay, see you on Sunday."

***

Bea and Pat were talking quietly about Claire's nightmare and how, since then, she had been afraid to sleep in her own room. Bea was wringing her hands and biting her lip. "I am at a loss what to do about her. I knew there would be problems with her, but she was fine for the first couple of weeks. She's getting worn down from lack of sleep and so am I. The tricks the therapist gave me don't seem to be working. We've established a routine and even bought her a white noise machine. I don't know why she keeps turning it off. When I ask her what's wrong, all she says is 'Man'."

Pat took Bea's hands in his and gently rubbed his thumb over the back of her wrist. "Bea, maybe we need to distract her more...get her mind on something else. I've been wanting to talk to you about this and I hope you agree…what do you think about getting her a dog? It would help her to share her emotions and she might feel more secure having a dog in her room at night. There are so many dogs at the SPCA looking for a good home. If we got one that was already housebroken, we wouldn't have to worry about doing that work. It would be good for her to have something to be responsible for."

Bea stared at him while she thought about his suggestion. Slowly, a smile spread across her face. "You know, we don't know when her birthday is. Why don't we have a party for her on Saturday and invite all the family? It doesn't have to be a birthday party, just a celebration. Do you think it is too close to Christmas to ask people to bring gifts? It would be the perfect time to give her a dog."

"I think it would be fine. Who knows what the next year will bring? It's always fun to buy toys for kids. I'm sure no one will mind."

***

Bea was bouncing on her toes with excitement. Brad had taken Claire to Dennis the Menace Park to play for a couple of hours and Pat was at the SPCA picking up a dog. The smell of fresh-baked cake permeated the rooms. "Thank you, Christina and Sue, for coming over to help me set up. The boys are coming in from college, but they won't be able to get here until later. Can you both put up some crepe paper streamers over the table? I have some balloons there too. Put them wherever you think they would look nice. Then we need to put silverware and napkins on the table. I'll keep the plates near the cake. Oh, I hope she likes the party. She has been so nervous and on edge lately. This should give her something happy to think about and show her how much she is loved."

They all turned as the door opened and Pat entered with a beautiful German Shephard. The dog was looking at her with his head titled to the side and his ears pointed up. The intelligent look in his dark eyes and his black face was endearing. He had a golden coat with a black, saddle like area on his back and a black nose. Across his forehead was a golden zig-zag like a lightning bolt. Bea approached him carefully and stretched out her hand for him to smell. When he licked her hand, she gently rubbed his neck.

"His name is Blaze," said Pat.

"With that design on his forehead, I can see why they named him that."

Patty and his girlfriend, June, followed close behind Pat with overnight bags and presents. Bea ran up to give them each a hug and then turned to Pat and the dog sitting patiently by his side. "I wasn't sure who to hug first...you, the dog, Patty or June. What a beautiful dog! I didn't expect one quite that big, but he does seem to be well behaved."

"They told me he is fully trained. He is only a couple of years old and doesn't have any health issues. His owner moved to assisted living and had to give up his dog. He was just too big for a little apartment. The dog's name is Blaze. I was lucky to be there just when he was being released for adoption. He's had all his shots and I brought home a bag of the dog food they suggested. Patty, would you go out to the car and bring it in with the bowls, brush and dog toys?"

Tom Kent entered with Patty as he returned with the dog necessities. "Hey Tom, good to see you! How come you are carrying the fifty-pound bag and Patty is carrying all the light things?" Pat reached out and took the bag from Tom and moved it into the garage.

"Where do you want me to put the gift for Claire?"

"Over there on the side table. Patty, you and the girls can put your things there too. Isn't this looking like a real party? Pat, take Blaze outside and show him where we want him to go to the bathroom. Maybe walk him around the property so he knows the boundary. Oh, look, Wally and Jerrod just showed up! Boys, park in the garage so Claire doesn't see your car. I doubt she would remember it, but I want it to be a surprise."

Bea took her phone and called Brad. "How's she doing? We are all here now, so whenever you want to come back is fine. Twenty minutes? Perfect. See you then."

"Okay everyone, they should be here in a few minutes. I don't think it would be a good idea to surprise her... she's been nervous enough lately. Pat, why don't you leave Blaze in the garage until she has seen everyone? Here's an old blanket for him to lay on. We can bring him in after she has opened her presents."

***

Claire came running through the front door and ran directly to Bea. Her face was flushed from playing at the park and her hair smelled like fresh air. After hugging Bea, she turned and noticed the balloons and streamers in the dining room. As she walked toward the table, the rest of the guests came up to greet her, one by one. When she looks quizzically at Bea, she put her arm around Claire and explained, "We all wanted to get together and throw a party to celebrate having you here in our family. All of us have come to love you and wanted to have a special day...just for you.

Claire looked around the room at each of the people who had become her family in such a short time. A look of unbelief crossed her face while her eyes filled with tears of joy. She buried her face in Bea's waist and sobbed.

"Oh dear. This isn't what I expected. We thought you would be happy." Taking Claire's face in her hands and turning it up to look at her, Bea said, "Claire, do you want everyone to leave?" Claire shook her head and a smile spread across her face as she wiped at her eyes with the back of her hands. She turned and went to each person and gave them a hug. Now, even the men had watering eyes as they were touched by this unusual show of affection.

"Ahem, well, (sniff), I think we should have some cake and ice cream to celebrate. What do you think? Claire, why don't you sit here at the head of the table?"

After the table was cleared of the empty plates and everyone was having a cup of coffee or milk, Pat started to bring over the gifts. There were markers, a drawing pad, crayons, scissors and many different craft articles. She had cleared an area near her seat and had already started drawing when Pat said, "Oh wait, Claire, I forgot that there is one more gift for you. Stay here and I'll be right back."

Pat went into the garage and brought Blaze into the room. Blaze stopped by the table and went to each chair and sniffed it. When Blaze got to Claire's chair, he sat down and laid his head in her lap. Claire's eyes were as round as saucers as she gently stroked the shepherd's fur.

"Claire, this is Blaze, he is going to be your dog. He is already housebroken and knows some basic commands, but you will have to work with him, feed him, walk him and brush him. We can help when you start school, but for now, you are responsible for him. Do you want to go outside and play with him for a little while?"

Claire grabbed the leash and led Blaze to the back door with most of the adults following behind her. It was a strange sight to see the little child easily leading the ninety-pound dog without any trouble. "First, you need to walk with him around the yard so he learns where our boundary is. We picked that corner in the back for him to go to the bathroom. You will need to scoop it up with this and then put it in a bag and into the garbage." Blaze sniffed a little and then squatted to show Claire that he already knew that this was his corner. They cleaned it up and then took him off leash so he could chase a ball. Since they had a fence around the backyard, there wasn't a problem with keeping him within the area. Claire would throw the ball and Blaze would bring it right back to her and drop it. However, when anyone else got in the game, he would bring it back, but then jump out of reach when they would try to get it back. If Claire clapped her hands, he would run back to her and drop it at her feet.

"I think we already know who he has chosen as his owner. They say that German Shepherds are very protective and usually latch on to one person in the family."

Christina linked her arm through Brad's and added, "That's true. We had a German Shepherd when I was a kid. He loved all of us, but Mom was his person. He would walk around the house at night to check on us, but would always go back and lay in front of her room."

Christina, Sue and June left together. "June you can stay with me while you are here. With Claire in the second bedroom, there isn't room for you here."

"Jerrod, you can crash on the couch or throw a sleeping bag on the floor of the boy's room. Is that okay?"

"Sure, Mrs. Oakley, I can sleep anywhere. I'm used to bunking with other guys."

After all the guests had left, Bea led Claire and Blaze to her room. "It's time for you to go to bed. We will let Blaze sleep in your room at night. See, I have already set up a bed for him to lay in. While you wash up and get your jammies on, I will get Blaze settled in his bed. Come here, Blaze. Lay down. Good boy."

Tucking the blankets around Claire, Bea was hopeful that having Blaze in her room would help the girl get over her nightmares. She needn't have worried since, the next morning, she found Claire laying on the ground, sound asleep, with her arm around the dog. Blaze lifted his head to see who was there and then laid his head back on the child's chest with a contented sigh.

23

Brad and Christina approached Keith Waldron's boat, The *Yknot*, in the harbor. The night was clear and calm. The moon was shining on the smooth water and the lights from the gathered boats were leaving colored reflections to highlight the beauty of the night.

"Permission to come aboard! What great weather for the parade this year, Keith, thanks for inviting us on board. Have you met Christina Velk? She is an ER doc at CHOMP and took care of me last year when I was poisoned and stabbed."

"Nice to meet you Christina. Welcome aboard. I still can't believe what happened last year. Those attacks were brutal. Thanks for taking such good care of Brad. Monterey is lucky to have him and we would all miss him. I guess I should say, we are really grateful to have you here, as well."

"Yes, it was a bad time, but unfortunately, I have seen worse in the ER. He was pretty lucky that he had rapid care both times. We're all happy he survived with very little after effects except for a scar."

Trying to move the topic off of himself, Brad asked,

"Do they think the wind will pick up tonight? It can get pretty cold at night when the wind blows across the cool water."

"It's supposed to stay calm. We have plenty of beverages on board to keep you warm. There's hot chocolate and, for the ones who want to imbibe, we have a sailors special, warm rum."

"Don't the sailors need to use their sails for the parade?"

"No, Christina, most of the boats have motors, so they won't need the wind to move in the parade. The sails would probably knock down the decorations. I think, next year, I may decorate my boat too. I was looking online at some other parades and they gave me a couple of ideas. Want to help, Brad?"

"That would be fun. However, my job often takes me away when I least expect it. I can't commit to something I can't follow through on. I haven't even been able to join you for the Wednesday sunset sails."

"Well, I can only hope. You are both always welcome. Why don't you grab a drink and snack? We'll be on our way soon."

Keith had a lively group of friends on board the *Yknot* and they moved out past the breakwater into the open bay. They could hear, and smell, the large group of sea lions as they went past the pile of rocks protecting the harbor. He put the boat in idle as they got into the bay and turned on some rollicking Christmas music.

"Oh listen, that was my dad's favorite Christmas song, 'Grandma Got Run Over by a Reindeer.' I can't say mom was thrilled with it, though!"

"Ha! I guess my family was more traditional with church songs on most of the time. There were a few years, when we were little, that Bea and I would sing, 'I saw Mommy Kissing Santa Claus.' Dad would wink at Mom and everyone would giggle when he went to her with a ho-ho-ho and a kiss."

Keith came over and held some mistletoe above their heads and everyone laughed when Brad gave Christina a peck on the cheek.

"Come on man, you can do better than that. Do you want me to show you how it's done?"

"No, that's perfectly okay. I'll show him how to do it." Christina leaned in and gave Brad a kiss that left him breathless and the group cheering.

"Look, the parade is starting!" When everyone rushed to the port side, Brad drew Christina to him and gave her another lingering kiss and then walked to the ship's rail with his arm around her waist.

"Look at that one! It looks like a porpoise jumping!"

"I like the one with the red Christmas tree."

"Ha, that one has a blow-up Santa and Snowman!"

"There has to be at least fifteen boats this year. It is so beautiful to see them silently gliding by. You can't hear the motors over the slapping of the waves. Look at all the people on the docks and shoreline watching the parade. What a beautiful night."

The silent parade was broken by a group on the shore singing "Jingle Bells". Soon the song was picked up by the people on Keith's boat and echoed back to the people on the shore. The magical moment was broken by the laughter and camaraderie of the onboard guests.

***

While the ships were circling the harbor, the Oakley family had taken Claire and Blaze to watch it from Cannery Row. In the few weeks he had been with them she'd become inseparable from the dog. People tended to take a wide path around Blaze, thinking that he would be aggressive. Little did they know what a sweetheart he was when accompanied by Claire. He looked adoringly at her and followed her every step. When people would get too close, he would gently place his body between Claire and them to let them know he was her protector.

Claire chuckled when she saw the statue in the Steinbeck Plaza adorned with Christmas hats on all the figures. Bea explained to Claire that the seven people were characters from John Steinbeck's novels and the man at the bottom of the monument was his friend, Ed Ricketts. While they found a place by the railing above the rocky shoreline, Bea explained, "John Steinbeck wrote about this area of Monterey. He grew up in Salinas and he wrote about the canneries and farms of the area. When you are older, they will probably teach you about him in school."

Bea was keeping a close eye on Claire as the neared the water. She remembered that her drawing with the art therapist showed that her home had been on a boat. She worried that seeing the boat parade might upset her. When they drew close to the railing overlooking the bay, Claire kept looking around her as if she was looking for someone. She held on to Blaze's collar to keep him close.

"Brad and Christina are on one of the spectator boats. Do you think you can see them? There are so many people in their boats, I'm not sure which one they are on."

Claire leaned closer to the railing when she saw the lighted boats appear on the water. She was intrigued by the different types of lights on the boats as they glided by. After the lighted boats had finished the course and turned to head back to the boat harbor, Claire yawned.

Bea noticed the gesture and said, "Did you enjoy the show? Wasn't it pretty seeing all those boats? I think we should go home and get this little one to bed."

***

Claire was snuggly tucked into her bed with Blaze on the ground next to her. Bea knew that, by morning, the dog would be laying in the bed with her or she would be on the floor with him. She didn't like the dog in Claire's bed, but it was if they couldn't sleep without that closeness. Bea kissed Claire on the forehead and gave Blaze a pat before turning out the light. "Sleep well you two. I'll see you in the morning."

As Bea cuddled in next to Pat she said, "I was worried about how Claire would feel being near the water and all those boats, but she seemed to enjoy it."

"You worry too much. Kids are resilient. It's hard to know what is happening in her head, but it probably isn't as bad as you think. Good night, sweetheart. Don't let the bed bugs bite you!"

***

As the town slowly quieted and the lights blinked off, the Oakley family was deeply asleep. Blaze lifted his head and tilted it from side to side. A low growl came from deep inside his chest. Suddenly, he leapt off the bed, barking ferociously, and put his paws on the windowsill.

The hackles on his neck were raised and he continued to bark while scratching at the window as if he were trying to get out. Pat Oakley ran into the room and threw on the lights to see what was happening while Bea went to Claire and wrapped her arms around her.

"What's out there? What do you see, boy? Come with me and we will check it out." Putting a leash on Blaze and going out the front door with a flashlight, Pat could just make out the figure of a person running down the block, while trying to restrain the dog who was pulling and leaping toward the disappearing figure.

"Bea, I think there was a prowler outside. Why don't you give Brad a call?"

"Is he gone? There isn't much we can do now. I doubt if he will come back tonight. Why don't we wait until morning and I will call him then."

"Okay, but I'm going to sleep in the room with her tonight."

"Do you really think you need to with Blaze in there? He did a great job of protecting her. What do you say, Claire? Do you want Pat to sleep in your room?"

Claire shook her head from side to side while hugging Blaze, who was licking her face. Haltingly she said, "Have Blaze."

"Okay, but if you change your mind, just come and get me. Good dog, Blaze. You keep an eye on Claire for us."

***

Brad rang the doorbell at the Oakley house and was shown into the kitchen by Pat. "Thanks for coming by, Brad. Would you like a cup of coffee and some Danish?"

"Sure. So, what's this about someone trying to get into the house last night?"

Handing Brad a cup of coffee and then sliding a plate in front of him, Pat said, "Last night, about one, we woke up to hear Blaze barking and growling at the window in Claire's room. When I went outside to see who was there, I saw someone running away."

"These are good! Did you get them at Paris Bakery?"

"Why didn't you call me last night? Did you get a good look at the person who was running away?"

"We needed a treat this morning after our scare last night. Bea bought them at Parker-Lusseau on Hartnell."

"I wanted to call, but Bea said it could wait until morning. No, I didn't get a good look at the person. It was dark and he was pretty far away already. I couldn't even see if it was a man or a woman. I don't think he, or she, will try it again after seeing Blaze in full protection mode. Do you think it has anything to do with Claire?"

Licking his fingers and wiping his hands on his jeans, Brad said, "It's possible that someone is looking for her, and not in a good way. Okay, let's take a look and see if there is anything we can find."

Walking outside, they stopped by the window into Claire's bedroom. "Somebody has definitely been here. There are footprints in the soil and some broken leaves on the bush. That cactus must have left at least a couple of stickers in the stalker." Looking at the ground, he added, "These footprints are pretty big. I would bet it is a man's print. Although some women have big feet too, I've never seen a woman with feet that big. I'll have the crime lab come over and take a cast of the print and see if they find any pieces of other evidence. It looks like he tried to pry open the window with something. Which direction was he running?"

"That way," Pat pointed toward the bay. "Like I said though, I didn't see much."

The men walked across the yard, noting footprints in the sandy soil, and then crossed the street where he probably ran. "I'll have a couple of police officers canvass the area to see if any of the neighbors has noticed anyone hanging around. I worry that Claire may have seen whoever killed her mother and that person is trying to eliminate a witness. We haven't found her father yet, so we can't count him out, but why would a father want to hurt his own child?"

"However, we all saw the scars and abuse she suffered before coming to us. I don't think a stranger did that to her. Of course, it could have been her mother that hit her, but she was also abused, so it was probably someone else. From what we have learned about her father, I wouldn't be surprised if he is the abuser."

"Look, there she is right now...and the hero dog. Hi Claire, hi Blaze." Claire stood by Pat while Blaze reached out to Brad and started licking his hand. Brad gently rubbed the big dog behind his ears.

"I bet he likes the taste of the Danish I ate!"

Claire smiled at Brad and pulled the dog back to her. With a simple hand signal, Blaze immediately sat at attention near her side.

"Wow, he is really well trained. Did you do all that?"

"No, he was already trained and Claire just taught him to respond to the hand signals she uses. He is a big dog and she is a little girl. If she didn't have complete control of him, he would pull her right off her feet. My dad had a dog that was hit by a car and was deaf afterwards. He responded to hand signals, so I thought we could do the same with Blaze until Claire starts to talk some more. She is saying more and more things, but only one word or two at a time. It is a great step in the right direction though It shows she is beginning to trust us."

Stepping to the side with Pat while Claire played with Blaze, Brad asked, "Has she said anything about the day we found her?"

"No, not yet. I know she misses her mother, and she has really become attached to Bea, but she doesn't say anything about before Bea found her in the church."

24

B rad sat at his desk reading the crime lab report. *Size twelve shoes. That's really big. Hmm, James' height is six foot six, so it's possible he would have shoes that big. Let's see if Tom has gotten any further with his inquiries.*

Brad caught Tom in the locker room as he was going off of shift. "Hey Tom. Did you get any further with your inquiries about Eliott James?"

"One of the older, neighborhood ladies, Mrs. Collett, had seen a tall man lingering on the street over the last few weeks."

"Did she have any description?"

"Mrs. Collett said he had light hair and was very scruffy looking. She noticed him because he ducked down behind a tree when the Oakley's car went by. She thought that was very strange. She said he was wearing jeans and an old navy type pea coat with a knit hat. Her late husband had been in the Navy during the Vietnam war, so she recognized the style of coat. I asked if he had pock marks on his face, but she said she was too far away to notice."

"I love nosey old ladies. They keep an eye on the

neighborhood and can be our best witnesses. Did she say when she saw him?"

"She said it was towards the beginning of December and she thought she saw him again in the evening a couple of times. It was getting dark though, and she couldn't be sure it was the same man. However, she was sure he was tall. By the way, she also makes a killer chocolate chip cookie. She gave me a box of them before I left. Want one?"

"No thanks, I'm sure they are great, but I am off chocolate chips since I was poisoned last year with one. My stomach flips just thinking of it."

"Sorry to hear that, but more for me." Tom grinned as he popped a cookie in his mouth.

"One more thing. When I was looking into James' background, I saw he had bought a boat when he was up in Oregon. I figured I'd check with the harbor master if any boats registered to Eliott James were in the harbor. It was a long shot, but since the mother and daughter had both been in the bay, I thought it was worth checking out. I went down there this morning after I talked to Mrs. Collett."

"And…what did the Harbormaster say?"

Tom swallowed another mouthful of cookie before answering. "No one by that name or description is registered in the harbor."

"Darn, I was hoping your idea led somewhere. Have you checked over in Moss Landing? The art therapist mentioned that she drew a boat when Claire was asked about where she lived. I'm glad you followed up on that idea. You'll make a good detective someday."

"It was just a hunch. I haven't checked Moss Landing yet. I've been busy with the prowler at your sister's place."

"Did you find anything else at Bea's house?"

"Well, the footprints were size twelve, which would go with a tall man. The treads were consistent with run-of-the-mill work boots. They look like the kind you can pick up at any Home Depot in the USA. I'll send the prints to the lab. There were some dark blue fibers on the cactus that match with the pea coat color and fabric that Mrs. Collett noticed."

"Good work, Tom. If he is in the area, he must be getting around somehow. Did anyone mention a strange car in the area? Can you check with the bus drivers and see if the Taxi, Lyft or Uber drivers have picked him up? If anyone gave him a ride or dropped him off at home, we can figure out where he is staying. Right now, we only have a description of a tall, light-haired man with big feet. It could be anyone, but my gut is telling me it's Eliott James."

25

It was a beautiful day in Monterey. The kind of day that makes one wonder if it really is December. While the rest of the nation was frozen under layers of snow and ice, California had turned green from the frequent rain storms. It was sunny with a light breeze and a comfortable sixty degrees. Bea had taken Claire over to Dennis the Menace park to play.

"Stand right there, Claire. I want to get a picture of you next to the statue of Dennis the Menace holding his teddy bear. I remember bringing my boys here when they were little. I'll have to get you one of the comics of Dennis. The artist who drew him, Hank Ketchum, used to live in this area. Dennis was basically a good boy who was always getting in trouble. They even made a film of his antics."

"When my boys were little, they were allowed to climb up on the big steam engine near the entrance. It's too bad they have it fenced off now. Sure, some kids might get hurt on it, but I think kids need to do things that are a little scary to build up their courage."

Claire had stopped listening and was climbing on one of the jungle gyms. Before Bea knew where she was, she had already climbed to the top and was waving. They had a great time going down the big slide, climbing, running and exploring. They even went over to watch the kids on the skateboard rink. It was encouraging to see how the older kids watched out for the little ones who were just learning the sport. Bea was beginning to get tired and hoped that Claire would be willing to go soon. She hated to take her away when she was so happy, but they needed to get home. Between the various apparatus, Bea could see her walking with a skip and swinging her arms as she twirled, trying to take it all in.

"Claire, we have to go now. I want to get home and start dinner for Pat. We have to walk back to the church lot where we parked our car. Are you ready? We will definitely come back here again."

Claire took Bea's hand in hers and swung it back and forth as they walked down Pearl Street toward Camino El Estero. Bea had Claire look both ways before crossing the street. When it was clear, Claire skipped ahead with Bea close behind.

"Claire, stay close. Cars don't always pay attention to people."

As Claire stopped and looked back, there was a screech of tires as a car pulled into the street and headed right for the girl. Bea ran and grabbed Claire and threw her to the side, just as the car crossed into the intersection, hitting Bea and sending her flying. Claire tumbled to the curb and froze when she saw Bea laying in the street. She hopped up and ran to where Bea was. She stared at Bea on the ground and looked around frantically for help.

Within seconds, other people ran to where they were. One called 911 and the others stood around wondering what to do.

"Don't touch her. There might be a neck or spine injury!"

"I have a pulse. Thank God she is breathing. Does anyone know her?"

"Is this her little girl?"

"Put this coat over her so she doesn't go in shock."

"What was that driver thinking? He didn't even slow down or stop."

Within minutes, they could hear the sirens from the Monterey Fire Department. Their garage was only a few blocks away and they got there quickly. They quickly moved to Bea's side and began administering first aid. They put a brace around her neck and began checking her vital signs. She did not open her eyes or respond to anything they were doing.

The police department is right next to the fire

department so a squad car showed up right behind the big rig. One officer got out to take witness statements and the other went over to talk to the firemen on the scene.

"She was run over by a hit and run driver. Maybe one of these people saw the car. Here is her ID."

"Oh no, this is Detective Brad Evan's sister, Bea. We better call him. This looks bad and he'll need to know. Is that her little girl? I heard they were foster parents."

It seemed like seconds before Brad showed up. He rushed to his sister's side as they lifted her into the ambulance.

"Hang in the Bea. Claire is okay. We'll take care of her and you are in good hands. I know you can't hear me right now, but I can't lose you. It would be like losing part of myself."

Claire rushed over to Brad and threw herself into his arms. She was sobbing uncontrollably and shaking with fear.

"It's okay honey. Bea will be alright. She has to be. There are too many people who love her and would miss her."

26

Brad was pacing back and forth in the family waiting room at the Community Hospital of Monterey when Pat rushed in.

"How is she? Come here Claire baby. How are you doing? It must have been horrible for you. Are you sure you are okay?" Pat pulled Claire to him in a one-sided hug.

"They did a quick exam on Bea and then rushed her up to surgery. Christina said she would come and update us as soon as there was news. "Pat," Brad said, his voice breaking. "I don't know what I would do without her. I'm sorry, this must be terrible for you too. How are you doing? I shouldn't bother you with my worries right now."

"Oh Brad, it's hard on all of us. I understand. She is a fighter and I know, God willing, that she will get through this. Why don't we sit down and say a little prayer for her?"

Brad, Pat and Claire sat down and held hands while they prayed. "Loving God, I know you love your children and you suffer with us. If it is your will, please bring our Bea back to us. Amen." A sob escaped his throat and Claire climbed into his lap and gave him a hug. Pat buried his face in her shoulder for a moment. Then he wiped his eyes and straightened his back. "I will not give up hope. I know she will come back to us."

"Pat, did you call the boys?"

"Yes, Wally is driving down and Patty will be flying in from UCLA with June. They are both going to come directly to the hospital. I don't think we will be out of here before they come."

Brad continued pacing and Pat sat dejectedly with Claire in the chairs set up for famioies. Soon, her adrenaline rush died out and she fell deeply asleep. He gently laid her down and got up to pace with Brad.

Tom Kent came into the room and put his hand on Brad's shoulder. "How is she doing?"

"We don't know anything yet. She is in surgery right now."

"I interviewed the witnesses and they all said it looked like the driver was heading directly for Claire when Bea shoved her out of the way and took the full brunt of the impact. The car didn't even slow down before racing away. Who would do such a thing?"

Gritting his teeth, Brad said, "I think I know. The same someone who tried to break into Claire's bedroom. If I ever get my hands on him, I don't know what I will do. Did anyone get an ID on the car?'

"Not much. It happened so fast. Everyone did agree that it was a dark grey, four-door car."

"Great, as if there aren't a million of them on the road. No one recognized the model or license plate?"

"Nope. No car buffs in the crowd, I guess. Just a bunch of moms with kids."

Tom put his hand on Brad's shoulder. "Hang in there. We'll cover things until you are ready."

Shaking hands with Pat and telling him how sorry he was that this happened to Bea, Tom then left to head back to the office.

As he exited the room, Christina Velk came in. Brad and Pat anxiously jumped to their feet.

"Christina, have you heard anything? How is she? No one is telling us anything."

Giving both men a quick hug, Christina answered, "She is seriously injured. She took a direct hit from the car. Her hip is broken, some ribs, and she has a concussion. Those can all heal. What concerns us is the internal bleeding and damage to her spleen. They are taking her to surgery. The doctors here are excellent and they will do everything they can for her. Right now, we just have to wait and see."

Pat collapsed in a chair and put his face in his hands. He gave out one shuddering sob. "I don't know what I would do without her. She is my life."

Christina sat down next to him and put a hand on his shoulder. "Don't give up hope. Like I said, the doctors here are great. She is a fighter and we have to be strong for her."

Claire woke up and looked sadly at the grownups. "Hello, Claire. How are you doing? Come over here for a minute, darling. Can I look at you to make sure you don't have any injuries?"

"Oh no! We were so concerned about Bea, we forgot to check if Claire was alright."

"That's understandable. Let me look at you. Does it hurt anywhere?" As Christina checked out Claire, she noticed some abrasions and bruises, but nothing serious. "Look in my eyes. Follow my finger. Can you move all your arms and legs? That's perfect. I'll get some ointment for your scrapes, but it looks like you are fine."

"Turning to Pat she said, "Bea is a hero. If it weren't for her, things would look very different for Claire. Her quick thinking saved her life. Now, we will try to save hers."

Brad walked her out the door. Quietly he asked, "Thank you for coming by. How bad is it really? Did you hold anything back from Pat?"

"No, her condition is serious, and we will do everything we can. I'll come back later to update you after the surgery." Christina leaned her head forward and gently touched foreheads with Brad. Then she took his face in both her hands, "Have faith. Don't give up on her."

27

Pat Oakley was sitting by Bea's bed, holding her hand and speaking softly to her.

"The boys are doing a great job taking care of the house and Claire. Of course, they are worried, but are doing their best to keep things normal for her. We are all looking forward to bringing you home again."

Brad was looking out the window at the massive Monterey pine and scrub oak trees that surrounded the hospital. Usually, he was mesmerized by the beautiful stillness surrounding the hospital. Today however, his mind was miles away. He felt as if he was walking through a fog. His usually sharp brain, moved sluggishly and continued to circle around morbid thoughts about Bea. *What if she doesn't make it? What if she is impaired somehow? How would I live without my sister?* When these thoughts arose, Brad tried to push them back into the fog, but they slowly seeped back into his mind. Shaking his head to clear these thoughts, he approached Pat.

"Why don't you take a break? I'll be here."

"Thanks, I really could use the chance to stretch my legs. I won't be gone long though."

"If you pass the coffee shop on the way, would you get me a cup of coffee? Black, no sugar."

Brad sat down in the chair by the bed. His head was down and his hands clasped. One of his legs was jiggling up and down. He would jerk occasionally and pace around the room before sitting back down again. The steady beep, beep, beep of the monitors and the mechanical sound of the pressure cuff inflating were the only sounds in the room. Occasionally, he could hear a bird outside in the oak trees, or the wind blowing through the branches. A soft murmur could be heard from the nurses at the station desk. It seemed so odd to him that the nurses and doctors were going about their daily routine while, everything in the world had changed in here. Bea's head had a bandage wrapped around it and her swollen face was covered with bruises. There was an intravenous line in her arm and he knew there were more bandages where they removed her spleen. Occasionally she would moan, but so far, she had not woken up.

It had been four days since the hit and run, and she was still out. Brad was deeply concerned. Seeing her laying on the bed, so badly injured, was like removing a piece of himself. They say that twins feel on a deeper level what the other twin is experiencing than with other siblings. Brad didn't know about that, since she was his only sister, but he felt like part of him had died.

Don't think that way! She is not dead. She will get better.

He sunk his head in his hands again. Over the sounds of the lunch cart in the hallway, Brad thought he heard a noise from the bed. Looking up, he saw Bea looking at him.

Bea croaked softly, "Brad."

"Oh Bea. It's good to see you awake again. Let me tell the nurse."

"What happened?"

"You were in a car accident. You are at the hospital. Do you remember anything?"

"No. Everything fuzzy. I remember being at the park with Claire."

"Claire is fine. You saved her life."

Bea smiled and dropped her head back on the pillow and closed her eyes. Brad rushed out to the nurses' station.

"She is awake! Bea is awake!"

They rushed into the room, but Bea had gone back to sleep.

"Did she say anything?"

"Yes, she seemed confused and didn't remember the accident. She asked about her little girl. When I told her she was okay, she smiled."

"That's good. It shows her cognitive function is intact. I will notify her doctor. Right now, the sleep is good for her. If she can sleep through the first days, she'll be over the worst of the pain. Her body is working very hard to repair the damage."

Pat walked in holding two coffee cups. "What's up?" He glanced over at the sleeping Bea.

"Bea woke up! She asked about Claire and then went back to sleep."

"What? What did you say?"

Brad pounded him on the back. "She woke up! She asked about Claire and then fell asleep again."

Pat let out a big sigh and then glanced heavenward. "Thank God! I was trying to stay positive, but a part of me thought she wouldn't make it. I should have had more faith. Bea is strong and wouldn't give up so easily."

Putting down the coffees, he went over to the bed and took Bea's hand. He leaned over and kissed her gently on the cheek.

"You sleep now, sweetheart, and then come back to us. We need you. I need you." A sob escaped his lips and then he wiped the tears of joy from his face. Brad came over and placed a hand on his back.

"Where's Claire? I think she'll want to know that Bea

is getting better."

"The boys are with her. They've been great. When did they get so capable? Even though they are worried, they are taking care of the house, the meals and babysitting Claire. She has been very upset about the accident and the boys and June have tried to keep her busy and her mind off of what happened."

"How are they doing?"

"Not too bad. Of course, they are worried. They love their mother, but that optimism of youth keeps them from going into a dark place. Being busy, caring for everyone else, has helped too. We all feel helpless, but they feel like they are doing something. I think it is harder for Claire, because she saw it happen."

Both men turned as Christina entered the room. "What's this I hear? Bea is awake?" She started looking at the monitors and checking the computer.

"Well, she woke up for a second and asked about Claire. When I told her she was alright, she went right back to sleep. She doesn't remember anything about the accident."

"Right now, she is under heavy sedation, so she may not remember everything. Her memory of the accident may come back, and it may not. She did remember Claire though, so that part of her memory is okay. Her vitals look great. I think we can cautiously hope for a full recovery. They had to remove her spleen, but people can live very well without it. She will just have to be more careful about infection. I know you all want to talk to her, but right now, sleep is the best thing for her. Her body is working hard to heal and she needs the rest."

Brad clenched his jaw and folded his arms across his chest. "I'm going to get whoever did this and lock him away for a very long time."

28

Wally Oakley came into Bea's hospital room, pushing a small child in a wheelchair. She had on a surgical mask and was covered in a blanket. Once Wally had closed the door and drawn the curtain to the entry, the child took off her mask and climbed down from the chair. She had a, slightly bent, nosegay of flowers in her hand.

"Claire! I was wondering why Wally was bring another patient into my room! Come closer, sweet cheeks. I know I look terrible, but I am okay. You don't need to be afraid."

Claire walked hesitantly to the bed and handed Bea the flowers.

"For me? Aren't these beautiful. I love flowers. Thank you so much for coming to visit me. Hi Wally, thanks for coming. It gets pretty boring, laying around all day. Can you get a vase from the nurses' station so Claire can put her flowers in water?"

"There, that's perfect. I can look at them all the time. They really brighten up this room. Thank you."

Leaning in to give his mother a kiss, Wally asked,

"Hi Mom, how are you doing? I hope we don't get caught sneaking Claire in here, but she really missed you and they don't allow children in here. So, we thought we would risk this ruse. I think your bruising is getting better. You don't look much like a prize fighter who was down for the count. It's starting to turn green. Maybe we should call you Shrek."

"Ha! Ow! Don't make me laugh. I may look and feel better, but I still have some stitches that hurt when I laugh."

Claire moved closer to the bed with her eyes down and her hands fidgeting. She lifted her eyes to Bea's face and then quickly looked down again.

"Oh darling. Come closer. I'm going to be alright. Don't worry. I know I look terrible, but it's just bruises. You've had them before. They will go away. I'm just glad that you aren't hurt." Bea tried to put her arm around the girl, but the one-sided movement made her jerk from the pain. "Come around here to the other side so I can give you a real hug. I missed you. Have you been having fun with Wally and Patty?"

Claire nodded her head and melted into Bea's arm around her. She gently touched Bea's head. The bandages had been removed, but her hair had been cut around the wound so they could stitch it closed.

"I look funny, don't I? When I get better, I will have to go and get a new haircut to even everything out. What I wouldn't give for a shampoo!"

Claire lifted up a drawing that she made. "Oh, my goodness! What a lovely drawing. There's the sun and flowers. Is that you and me standing on the grass? Thank you so much. Wally, can you put it over there by the flowers so I can see it all the time." Squeezing Claire again, Bea kissed her on the head.

"Now, Wally, what's the news from the outside world?

"Patty and I never realized how much work there is to keep a house running. The meals, laundry, cleaning, shopping and so forth. I will certainly be more appreciative when you get back home."

"You know, when I get home, I will still not be up to full speed. I'll still need some help. I haven't heard yet when I will be released from here. My physical therapist is wonderful and I am getting around fairly well. I know you boys will have to go back to school. Can you check with the church if there is someone that could come and help out for a while when I come back? Has Claire been taking care of Blaze?"

"She sure has, haven't you, Claire? She walks him every day and cleans up after him. She likes to brush that shaggy coat too. I think Blaze likes all the attention."

Giving Wally a somber look, Bea said, "I hope you

aren't letting her walk him by herself?"

"Of course not. One of us goes with her every time. No one will mess with our little sister with Blaze and us protecting her." Bea's heart melted when she heard Wally refer to Claire as his little sister. She thanked God that she was so blessed to have such good sons.

Claire went over to Wally and leaned both her forearms on his leg. He reached down and tussled her hair. She climbed up to sit in his lap.

A petite, young, woman with dark hair pulled back in a ponytail, peeked in the doorway. "I don't mean to interrupt, but it's time for Mrs. Oakley's walk."

"Come in Sally. I thought I told you to call me Bea?"

"I know, it's just a habit, Mrs., I mean, Bea."

"This is my son, Wally, and my foster child, Claire. Guys, this is my physical therapist: wonder worker, slash, torturer, Sally."

Wally stood up to shake her hand and stared into her eyes. It seemed to Bea that held on a little too long before letting go.

"Nice to meet you, Sally. I hope my mother isn't giving you a hard time."

"Of course not! She is the perfect patient. She never complains and works hard."

"Yup, that sounds like her. Well, we better get going and leave you to it. Come on Claire. Give Bea a kiss and then we have to go. I hope I'll see you again sometime, Sally."

Blushing, she answered, "I'd like that."

29

Christina Velk walked into Bea's room to see it filled with her family. "I'm glad you are all here. I have some good news for you all. Bea is doing so well that we want to send her home tomorrow. She will still need physical therapy, but she is getting around well enough that she can be released. It is very important that she continue with her exercises and follows up with her doctor. If there are any signs of infection, she needs to contact her physician immediately. They will give her more thorough instructions tomorrow, as well as, a script for medications. It's a good thing your house is one story. It will make it much easier for her to walk around. It would help if you picked up any throw rugs so she doesn't trip on them."

"Thank you, Christina! That's great news. Even though everyone here has been wonderful, there isn't anything better than sleeping in my own bed."

***

Pat pulled the car into the driveway and ran around to the other side. After unfolding her walker, he helped Bea stand up.

"Stop hovering around me! I've walked the whole length of the hospital. This walker is more for security than to help me walk. A fall at this stage could be very dangerous and this contraption should prevent me doing that. Open the door and stand out of the way so I can get in."

"Claire, grab Blaze. We don't want him running into Bea and knocking her over!"

Claire ran into the house and grabbed Blaze by the collar, dragging him back into the living room. She held onto him and had him sit.

"Okay, now the coast is clear and you can come in. Come over here and sit in the recliner. Do you want to put your feet up? Do you need a lap quilt? How about something to drink? I'll go over to Ordway in a minute to pick up your medicine."

"When did you become such a mother hen, Pat? I'm fine. I will sit for a bit though. It's amazing how good I felt in the hospital and how tired I am from just a little car ride."

"We forget that our bodies are constantly adjusting to the movement of the car. After lying still for weeks, you aren't used to it."

Claire brought Blaze over to see Bea, but kept a firm grip on his collar. Bea reached out her hand to pet him.

"Hi Blaze, good boy. Claire, you are doing a great job

of training Blaze. Look how well he listens to you. I like the red ribbon in your hair. Was that your idea? "Claire pointed toward June who reached out to stroke her hair.

"Are you happy to have me home? I know the boys have been spoiling you while I've been away."

Claire nodded her head so hard it looked like it would break off.

"Is that a, yes, you missed me or a yes, the boys spoiled me?"

Claire pointed at Bea.

"Well thank you. I missed you too. I missed all of you." Bea looked around at Pat, Wally, Patty and June. Her eyes misted a little when she thought of how much they meant to her. Bea still didn't remember much of the accident. She remembered seeing the car and pushing Claire away, but beyond that, she didn't remember anything until she woke up in the hospital. Brad had filled her in on the rest of the story. She found it hard to believe that someone was purposely trying to run them over. Thank God her guardian angel was protecting them.

"Well, enough of this. I'm here. I'm going to be alright and let's move on with our lives. Pat, I will take that quilt you offered and then I may take a little nap. The sun on this chair is nice and warm. No, no, don't close the curtains. I like it. CHOMP has beautiful views out the windows, but I missed sitting in the sun. *Yawn*. Wake me for lunch, okay?"

The rest of the family each gave her a kiss and then moved quietly away. Bea closed her eyes. She could hear the murmur of their voices in the next room. Her last thought before falling asleep was, how good it was to be back with her family."

30

B rad and Tom were going over the chart of events since they found the body of Stephanie Goodwin. Brad was tapping a pencil against the desk while Tom riffled through the papers again.

"I keep feeling like we are missing something. We're pretty sure it is Eliott James who is responsible for the murder and, most likely, the hit and run, as well as, the attempted break in at the Oakley house. Tom, did you check on the boats in Moss Landing?"

"I've called a couple of times, but I never got a hold of anyone. I'll go over today to check on it."

"I'll go with you. At least it will feel like I'm doing something. I want to get this guy. I can only believe that he isn't done trying to get to Claire. I'll never forgive myself if he slips through our fingers."

Grabbing their coats, they headed out toward Moss Landing. The twenty-five-mile drive was uneventful. Across the Bay they could see the five-hundred-foot towers of the power plant in Moss Landing. Even though they weren't in use anymore, they were an iconic symbol of the town. They hit the usual pockets of traffic near Sand City where everyone slows down to look at the bay between the sand dunes and again when Highway One veers off to the left toward Santa Cruz.

"The Salinas River is really full this year. It's nice to see after the drought we had the last few years. The weather guys on KSBW predict we will have enough rain and mountain snow this year to get us back to normal water levels."

"I heard that too. At first, I was happy to see all the rain, but now, I'm getting a little tired of the constant downpours." Brad turned into the sandy parking lot in front of the Harbormasters office.

"Here we are. Let's check in with the Harbormaster to see if he has registered a boat from Eliott James."

Entering the Harbormaster's office, Tom and Brad walked up to the counter and rang a bell to get someone's attention. From the back a female voice said, "Be right with you."

From the back room a woman with long hair just beginning to show a few strands of grey and wearing dirty, faded, jeans overalls, came out while wiping her hands on a rag. "What can I do for you gents? I was just cleaning up after gutting some fish for dinner so I won't shake your hands."

"I am Detective Brad Evans and this is Officer Tom

Kent." They both took out their identification and showed them to the woman behind the counter.

"Nice to meet you both. I'm Gladys Jones. I am the Harbormaster here. What can I do for the constabulary of Monterey?" She pulled off her dirty gloves and stowed them under the counter.

"Well, we are looking for someone who may be living on a boat in the area. Have you had anyone named Eliott James register here?"

"Hmm, doesn't ring a bell, but let me look in the book. When would he have been in the area?"

"We think he came a couple of weeks before Thanksgiving."

As she continued to look through the registrar, Gladys said, "I wasn't here at that time. My daughter had a baby down in LA and I went down to help her out. Nope, nobody by that name registered here. I guess you could try up in Santa Cruz."

"That's an idea, but I doubt if he is that far away. If you hear anything, here is my card."

"Wait, what does he look like? Maybe I've seen him around."

"James is over six feet tall and has a pocked marked face."

"A lot of the guys here are tall, but the face should stand out. I haven't seen anyone like that, but I'll keep an eye out. Why are you looking for him?"

"I can't talk about that now. It is an ongoing investigation. Thanks for your help."

Brad and Tom walked back toward their car and stopped to watch the sea otters playing in the water.

"Tom, want to catch a quick bite at the Moss Landing Café? My treat."

"If you put it that way, I'm in. I've been dying for some fried artichokes."

As they settled into their seats and ordered a double portion of artichokes, Brad and Tom discussed the case.

"It was good to get out of the office and do a little field trip, but it sure didn't get us any further in finding James."

"He must be using an alias, but you'd think that someone would notice a guy like that."

***

Gladys turned toward the man coming out of the back room. "You didn't tell me the police were looking for you."

Putting his arms around her and nuzzling her neck, James replied, "Aw, sweet thing. It's nothing to worry about. My ex-wife probably made another bogus complaint about me. She's one taco short of a combo plate. That vindictive hag is always finding some way to make my life miserable. If she were half the woman you are, I would still be married. Now come here and give me some of that sweet sugar you have."

James led Gladys by the hand into the back room where a bed was waiting.

31

Christina looked into the mirror and rearranged her hair. First, she drew it up on top of her head and then let it fall around her face. She knew that Brad loved her hair. It was thick and lustrous and one of her features she also liked. *Yes, I definitely will wear it down tonight. It's been awhile since we have gone out. He has been completely wrapped up in this case. Who can blame him? This one is very close to home. I am so relieved that Bea is doing well. Little Claire is a doll. Considering all she has been through; it is amazing that she doesn't display more signs of disturbance. Having Blaze to protect her has been a godsend. She is very clingy now with Bea since the accident. No wonder. That must have been terribly frightening for her.*

***

The doorbell rang and Christina went to let Brad in. He had a large poinsettia plant in his arms.

"I thought this might help get you in the holiday spirit. After Christmas, you can try planting it outside. Sometimes they grow. I've never had any luck, but you might."

"Thank you, Brad. It's lovely. I'll put it over here by

the fireplace. I haven't had much time to decorate, so this will get me started on the festive mood of the season."

"Where are we going tonight?"

"Have you ever been to a Tuba Christmas? I went last year and it is a lot of fun."

"No, I haven't. What is it? I assume tubas are involved."

"Exactly. Once a year, anyone who plays a tuba can join the orchestra and play Christmas songs for an hour or so. We better get going because it gets really crowded. Here, I brought you a Santa hat to wear."

So much for getting my hair just right!

As the entered the Monterey Conference center next to the Portola Hotel, they saw hundreds of people streaming into the building. Everyone was smiling and a general air of excitement filled the air. As they entered the large conference room, they were surprised to see at least a thousand people already in their seats. They eventually found two seats together and settled in with their programs.

Brad and Christina both recognized several people in the crowd and waved to them across the room. "Oh look, there's Tom and Sue. I didn't know they were coming tonight. We could have done a double date. Sue! Tom! Darn, they didn't see me."

"Actually, I'm glad they didn't. It's been a long time since we have been out together, just the two of us. I was hoping we could be alone tonight. It's not like we don't see them at work all the time."

Linking her arm through his, Christina answered, "You are right, this is much nicer. Oh, look, here come the musicians."

"Wow, there must be over sixty tubas on the stage."

One of the organizers came out to greet the crowd and introduced the director of the orchestra. She explained that the conductor goes all over the USA organizing tuba events. Except for a quick practice beforehand, most of the musicians had never played together before. They had practiced the Christmas Carols earlier in the day and that was all the preparation they had. Over the course of the evening the conductor described the different types of tubas and also introduced some of the musicians. Some were just starting out in their school bands and some had been playing for a lifetime. One group was an entire family of tuba players.

The audience was encouraged to sing along to the songs and everyone had a rollicking good time. When it was over, Brad and Christina tried to sneak out without Tom and Sue seeing them.

As they walked to the car, they chatted about the

various types of instruments they saw. "Remember the one that dates all the way back to the Civil War? That was so interesting how it faced backwards so the troops could hear the music while they marched."

"Some of them were huge and then there was the little "pocket tuba". I don't think I ever knew there were so many sizes and shapes."

"Thank you, Brad, for bringing me. It definitely got me in the Christmas mood. I had a great time."

"Well, let's keep it going then. I have another seasonal treat for you. I thought we could go over to Candy Cane Lane in Pacific Grove to see the Christmas decorations. The whole neighborhood gets together and decorates their houses. I have been going to see it since I was a little kid."

"Great. I can't wait to see it."

As they approached Candy Cane Lane, the cars were lined up trying to drive through the area.

"Why don't we park here and walk. We can see more and move faster than in the car. It isn't that cold tonight. Okay?"

"Sure. I'm game for anything, as long as it is with you." Christina's smile melted Brad's heart and they held hands as they got out to walk.

As they turned the corner, they could hear various

Christmas songs being played throughout the neighborhood. Some of the yards had every inch decorated with lights, while others had large, cut-out plywood figures of elves, Santas, candy canes and lollipops. In a little pocket park area, there was even a carousel with children on it. They bought an apple cider and stood watching the carousel for a while.

Brad felt a tap on the shoulder. "Brad, I thought that was you. Hi Christina."

"Oh, hi Tom."

"We thought we saw you at the Tuba Christmas, but couldn't catch your attention. I'm glad we caught up to you here. Oh look, there's Patty, June and Claire! Hey, over here!"

"Oh, hi guys. Good to see you. It's a real family gathering. Bea wanted to rest so we thought we would bring Claire over to see the lights. Wally is out with Sally somewhere. I hated to see Bea get hurt, but it was a lucky day for Wally. He is really crazy about Sally."

"That is nice for him. Claire did you see the house with the blue lights and the big Elvis singing 'Blue Christmas'?" Claire looked at Christina like she didn't know what they were talking about.

"You know, Elvis Presley. The singer? Big sideburns?

Doesn't ring a bell for you, does it. He was a singer a long time ago. Even before I was born, but his music were classics and are still played all the time. He was quite popular with everyone, but mostly the girls."

"I think they liked him because of the way he swung his hips around."

Christina and Sue both punched Patty lightly on the arm. "You don't need to tell her that. She's just a kid."

Pouting and rubbing his arms, Patty said, "Well, it's true." He quickly jumped away before the girls could punch him again.

Brad grabbed Christina's hand saying, "We ought to get going if we are going to make it to that other thing tonight."

Looking at him quizzically and then nodding her head. "That's right. I was having so much fun, I forgot about the other thing. We better run."

Running away like too naughty school children, Brad and Christina left the others shaking their heads and wondering what happened.

"Would you like to go out to the Mission Inn to have a drink. I haven't seen Clint Eastwood there for a while, but he sometimes shows up to play piano.

"I have a nice bottle of wine at home if you would

rather come to my place."

"That would be great. With our luck tonight, my dead parents will show up next to hang out with us. Who knew we were so popular?"

***

Brad and Christina were sitting on the couch in her living room looking at the moon shining through the trees. They could hear the waves on the shore and gentle music was playing in the background. Two Santa hats were lying on the coffee table and Brad rested his arm on the back of the couch while he gently played with her hair. Setting down his wine glass, he slowly turned her face toward him and gave her a long, lingering kiss. She placed her hands on each side of his face and kissed him back. Finally, she asked, "Would you like to stay over tonight?"

Brad pulled back and expressions of panic, fear and chagrin crossed his face. "I, uh, I don't think so. Not tonight."

"I thought you felt the same way I do." Christina said with a break in her voice.

Brad took both her hands in his. "I do, I mean, I really care for you. Maybe I am falling in love. The trouble is, after last year, I'm not sure what I am feeling. I thought I was in love then and looked what happened. I just need a little more time. I hope you can understand."

Christina dropped her hands and walked to the window. After a minute she turned around. "Thank you for being honest with me. I understand what you are saying and I am willing to wait for you to figure it out. However, I won't wait forever. You know how I feel and I hope you know I am nothing like Maria."

"My heart knows that, but my mind keeps telling me to be careful."

"Well, I think you should probably go now. If you can't trust me, then I don't know if we can survive as a couple. You know where I am if you figure it out."

She turned back toward the window and he slowly grabbed his jacket from the hall and let himself out. As the door closed behind him, he could hear a sob on the other side.

32

Bea pulled into the driveway and slowly climbed out of her car. She reached around and pulled out her walker before hobbling into the house. Closing the door while balancing her purse and trying to keep both hands on the walker was difficult and she dropped the purse on the side table as soon as she got inside. Blaze greeted her at the door, jumping in front of her with excitement, but stayed out of the way. Claire had trained him not to jump on people. Bea limped into the family room and dropped into a recliner.

She could feel all the muscles in her body start to relax as she slowly sank deeper and deeper into the chair. She pulled her favorite afghan over her lap, closed her eyes and leaned back. Blaze lay down next to her and she put a hand on his head, brushing the soft fur with her fingers. Her mind was racing, but started to grow calm as she relaxed.

"You're a good boy, Blaze. You always act as if I have been gone for weeks when I come home. I'm glad we taught you not to jump on people. It would be hard if you knocked me over in your eagerness to see me."

Bea turned in her seat as she heard a noise at the front

door. Blaze rose to his feet and trotted toward the front door.

Brad knocked on the door and opened it slightly. "Bea, it's me, Brad. Are you home?"

"What? Oh, Brad! I'm back here in the family room."

Blaze stood at attention when he saw Brad and wagged his tail. "You recognize me, don't you Blaze. Good boy." Brad rubbed Blaze on the head and walked over to his sister and gave her a hug. "Don't get up. That Blaze sure is a good dog. Are you sure he will protect you if you need it? He was so calm when I came in."

"You didn't see him when the intruder was at Claire's window. I don't have any doubt he would attack anyone who tried to hurt me or my family. He probably recognized you somehow. He just knows when he has to behave. He is even good about staying out of my way so I don't trip. Would you mind letting him outside for a potty break?"

When Brad and Blaze returned, Brad asked, "How are you feeling?"

"Ha! I didn't know there were so many places on my body that could all hurt at once. The good thing is that I can see a steady progression of improvement. Today I even drove myself to my physical therapy appointment. It was tiring, but I know it is making me stronger. Each time I go, I feel stronger. So, overall, I'm good."

"How can you stay so positive? I would be angry on top of the pain."

"I read something once that I try to keep in mind: 'Can you do something about it? Yes? Then do it and don't worry. Can you do something about it? No? Then don't worry.' No matter what situation we are in we can choose how we react. It was terrible what happened, but I survived, Claire is okay and I am healing. I refuse to let it get me down. I can hurt, but I refuse to suffer. If anything, it makes me realize how lucky I am. I have good doctors, a loving family and a comfortable home to recuperate in. Now, let me play the invalid card once more and ask you to make us some coffee. I think there are still some snacks in the kitchen too."

"I live to serve. Be right back."

Brad came back, balancing a tray with two cups of coffee and a plate with some fruit and cheese.

"I thought you would go for the cookies in the jar. They are really good."

"I just don't seem to have a taste for cookies since I was poisoned last year."

"You know that won't happen again, don't you? I promise they are okay. We have all been eating them."

"I know, and I am sure I will get over it. Fruit is better for us anyway."

Barbara Siebeneick

"You are probably right. All this sitting around isn't helping my waistline much."

"Where are the boys? Where is Claire?"

"The boys had to go back to school for their semester finals. They'll be back in a few days. In the meantime, one of the ladies from the church stops by each day to see if I need anything. Claire helps run and fetch things for me and Pat cooks and helps with the cleaning, so overall, I'm well taken care of."

"Claire is at Mrs. Collett's house. She went there while I was at physical therapy. She should be home soon. Claire is such a sad little thing. She can laugh, but underneath there is this current of silent sorrow. She has been through more than most adults, let alone children. As much as we try to make her feel safe and secure, there are always things that drag her back down – like this accident."

"You know it wasn't an accident, don't you? That car sped up and headed straight for Claire. If it wasn't for you, she would have probably been killed. All the witnesses agree that it looked intentional. I would bet anything that it was Eliott James again. Speaking of which; why was your door unlocked? Anyone could have walked right in. It isn't safe."

"I know. I just got home and forgot to lock it after

myself when I came in. I will be more careful. However, I I'm sure Blaze would protect me with his life, if he needed to. Now, as flattered as I am that you came to visit the bedridden, why are you really here?"

Brad took a sip of his coffee. "You always seem to know how I am feeling. It must be a twin thing, although I don't seem to have the same sixth sense as you."

"I guess I just wanted to talk about Christina. I like her. I like her A LOT. She is ready to move the relationship forward, however, I'm not sure what I want. I don't want to lose her, but I really have trust issues since last year with Maria. I thought I was in love then and look how that turned out. But, without Christina, I am miserable."

"Come on, Brad. You know that Christina isn't anything like Maria. I was uneasy about Maria from the beginning, but with Christina I have only good feelings. Call it woman's intuition, but I think she is a keeper. Not every woman you date is going to hurt you so badly. What is it you like about Christina?"

"I know, I know. She is wonderful. Caring. loving, intelligent and beautiful. Maybe not beautiful in the classic sense, but she looks perfect to me. I know it's funny, but the thing I love the most is her hands. Every time I look at them, they remind me of all her good qualities. They are strong, but gentle, precise, yet playful. When she holds my hand, I actually feel a tingle. I've never had that feeling with a woman before."

"It sounds like you have already made up your mind. Just trust your instincts. She will understand if you want to take it slow. But don't be too slow. She might get tired of waiting."

"That's the same thing she said! Thanks for the advice. It really helped me clear my mind. Let me put this all away and then I better get going. Is there anything else you need? I'll lock the door on my way out."

"Oh, before you go, can you pick up Claire from Mrs. Collett and then lock the door? Someone told me that it isn't safe to leave it unlocked. Love you, Brad."

"You too, sis."

33

Eliott James slipped quietly out of bed without waking Gladys. He checked the time on his phone. *Midnight, plenty of time to get there and be back before she wakes up.* He grabbed his pants and shoes off the ground and dressed quickly in the harbormasters office before heading outside. He pulled his car out of the shed next to the dock and headed out onto Highway One toward Marina. This time of the night there were barely any cars on the road. There was a heavy fog that left a mist on the windshield and a haunted feeling over the Elkhorn Slough.

It only took a short time before James was pulling behind some of the old, abandoned buildings of Fort Ord. The old army base had been closed in 1994 due to Base Realignment and Closure by the government and was slowly being turned into shopping malls, a State University and housing developments. The cost of removing the asbestos from the decrepit buildings slowed the inevitable progress of total eradication.

James moved his car until it was facing out toward the exit and turned off the lights. He checked to make sure his gun was loaded and the safety latch was off. He stuck it in the back of his pants and stepped outside. He leaned against the car and looked toward the road he had entered.

Always better to be safe. The guys I am meeting here may be a bunch of teenagers, but that doesn't mean they aren't dangerous. Kids that age never think anything can happen to them so they are fearless.

James saw a lowrider car approach with its radio blasting a thump, thump, thump, that made his chest hurt. He wondered how these kids weren't all deaf. They pulled up and shone the car lights right in his face. Putting his hand up to shield his eyes, he could make out five forms emerging from the darkness and stepping in front of the car. They were only shadows, but he could make out the pants hanging low on their hips and the way they all had their hands on something in their waistbands. Someone in the middle of the group stepped forward.

"What you want with us? Word is you wanted to meet."

"I do. Enrique, up in San Jose said to talk to Francisco if I wanted to get some Oxy and guns."

"Maybe I am and maybe not. Do you mean Enrique Alvarez?

"Hell no, it was Enrique Martinez I talked to."

The head gang member nodded to one of his guys who

walked slowly forward and patted James down. He found the gun in the back of his pants and confiscated it.

He walked back with a wide legged stance that kept his pants from falling down. He nodded at the gang leader. James thought the baggy, hanging pants looked ridiculous, but he assumed they thought it made them look tough.

"I'm sure you understand that we can't be too careful. The cops are cracking down on the gangs in the area and looking for any excuse to bust us."

"That's cool. Just part of the cost of doing business these days."

"So, maybe I can get you some Oxy. How much do you want?"

"Not much. A hundred pills should do it. I'm also looking for a pistol. Preferably, a Glock .40."

"We can do the Oxy, but I don't have any Glocks right now. I can get you a 9mm semiautomatic though."

"That'll do. Do you have it on you?"

"Do you think I'm crazy man? I can get it to you in three days. Together it will cost you $4,000."

"Sure. I'll be back with the money on Wednesday night. Same time. Can I have my gun back?"

"Okay, but don't try anything stupid." The gang

member who had the gun, took out the bullets and threw them in the back seat of the car, before handing the gun back to James.

James stepped back cautiously as the gang got back in their car and drove away. Unconsciously, he let out a sigh of relief as he put the key in the ignition. He stretched his arm behind him and gathered the bullets from the back seat and put them back in his gun. He sat with his hands on the steering wheel for a couple of seconds before reaching over and starting the engine.

34

Bea let Blaze out in the backyard while she and Claire folded laundry.

"This pile of laundry never seems to get any smaller. Claire, hold the end of the sheet and help me fold it. Flat sheets are easy, but let me show you a trick with the fitted ones. Take the corner and fold it into the other corner. Now, take those corners and fold them into the one the first one. Lay it down and you have a nice square that can be folded again until it is flat. See? Now, let's put all the sheets from that bed into the pillow case. Now we can always find them together when we are ready to change the bed."

She watched the young girl working on folding the sheets. Her blond hair was, once again, pulled up in a pert little pony tail. She had put on weight since being with Bea and the haggard, starved, appearance had disappeared. Today, she looked like any other girl her age. Holding up a pair of Claire's tights, Bea laughed to think she had ever been that small. A pair of Claire's jeans would fit in one leg of Bea's slacks. *Well, it's not the size of the body, but the size of the heart that counts.*

Claire dropped the socks she was matching and went

to the window. She turned back to Bea with a questioning look on her face.

"What's going on? Why is Blaze barking? Is he barking at the crows in the trees or is there a squirrel teasing him?"

Bea hobbled over to the window in time to see Blaze charging the fence, barking madly, with his hackles raised. "What's going on? Oh no, Claire, run to the back door and make sure it is locked. Is the front door locked too? Good. Stay here with me while I call Brad."

"Come on, come on, pick up the phone. Hello Brad, it's Bea. Someone is trying to get into the yard. Blaze is keeping him at bay. Yes, I saw a leg come over the fence and Blaze bit into it. Please hurry. Claire is with me."

"Okay Claire, just stay with me. Brad is on the way and Blaze will protect us until he gets here. Let's move into the hallway where no one can see us through the window."

Bea crawled back into the room and peeked around a corner of the curtain. She gestured at Claire to stay hidden. Looking out, she saw Blaze take a huge leap and jump over the six-foot fence. Since there wasn't anything to see in the backyard anymore, she huddled in the corner with Claire until she heard a gunshot and then the squeal of tires.

"Stay here, don't move. I'll be right back."

Claire curled into a ball in the corner, but popped up and followed Bea as soon as she was out of sight. She grabbed Bea around the waist.

"Claire, you gave me a fright. I thought I told you to stay put. Oh, honey, don't cry. I'm not mad. You just scared me. I can hear the police siren. Thank goodness, they are so close. I think we are safe now."

Bea and Claire moved slowly to the front door, but didn't unlock it until they were sure that Brad was outside.

"Oh, Brad, thank you for coming. It was frightening. Thank goodness Blaze was there to protect us. Did he chase the intruder? Did you see him?"

"Yes, I saw Blaze. He has been shot. Don't worry, Tom's already got him in his car and is taking him to the vet. Are you both okay?"

"Yes, except for being frightened. Do you think it is James?"

"Probably. Did you see anything that could help us? His car? His face?"

"No, I'm sorry. I just saw the leg coming over the fence before I grabbed Claire to hide. Thinking of which, he did have big feet. Blaze had ahold of his pants and they were jerking around so much it was hard to see anything else. I didn't venture out until I heard the siren on your car."

"Well, hopefully, Blaze did some damage and he will have to go to the hospital for stitches. It would be a good break for us. I'll notify the hospitals in the area to be on the lookout for dog bite victims. I'll have someone ask the neighbors if they saw anything and I'll start some patrols of the area."

"Do you need anything else from us? Can you drive us over to the vet so we can be with Blaze? Pat can pick us up from there. Do you want to go see Blaze, Claire? Yeah, me too."

∗∗∗

Bea and Claire were impatiently sitting in the waiting room of the veterinarian clinic. Claire was distracted by the many animals waiting to be cared for by the veterinary staff. She cringed when she saw a black snake in a cage, but her curiosity overcame her fear and she approached cautiously.

"Hi there. Are you interested in my snake? We found him in our garage and thought we should bring him in to see what kind of snake it is. See the long stripe on its side? I think it is a garden snake. They are very helpful and not at all dangerous, but we want to make sure before we release it back in the yard. We wouldn't want to release anything that might hurt our other pets."

Claire smiled at the snake owner and wandered over to a woman who had a little puppy. She crouched down and looked up at the adult to seek permission to play with the dog.

"Sure, go ahead, honey. This is Herbie. He is just a couple of months old and we are bringing him in to make sure he has all his shots. You can play with him. Be careful though. He doesn't bite, but he might nip you with his little baby teeth. They are sharp, but it would only be for play. See how soft the bottom of his feet are and his cute little baby belly? I just love puppies. I wish they would stay like this forever. Uh oh, maybe not. I'll get some rags to clean up the mess he just made."

As the dog owner cleaned up the pool of urine, she said to Claire, "At least older dogs are house broken. Puppies will sometimes make a mess just because they are excited. He hasn't learned yet to tell us when he needs to go outside."

"Mrs. Oakley, you can come back now to see the doctor."

Bea and Claire quickly rose and followed the nurse into a small room in the back. They could see Blaze lying quietly on a table with a big bandage on his shoulder. Claire, immediately walked over to the table and gently stroked his back. She was careful to stay away from the bandaged area. When he didn't respond in any way, she turned her face toward the doctor with a concerned look.

"Don't worry, darling, Blaze is a very lucky dog. The bullet went cleanly through his shoulder without hitting any vital organs. Right now, he is still sleeping from the drugs we gave him before we took out the bullet. Just an inch the other way and he may not have made it. He lost a lot of blood, but he will be fine."

"Oh, thank you doctor. He was so brave, fighting off the intruder at our house. I would feel awful if he died trying to protect us."

"Well, he won't be doing any fighting for a while. I want to keep him here for a couple of days to make sure there isn't any chance of infection and to give him an IV to replace the blood he lost. You can pick him up the day after tomorrow."

35

"Tell me again how this happened?" Gladys was cleaning the dog bites on Eliott's leg.

"Ow!"

"Don't be such a big baby. The bites aren't that deep. So, what's the story?"

"I already told you once. I was walking on the rec trail and a lady passed me with her pit bull. Out of nowhere, he lunged at me and bit my leg. He got in a couple more bites before she pulled him off me."

"Why didn't you call the police and report it? A dog like that shouldn't be allowed to roam around."

"You know me, she begged me not to turn him in and I just can't stand to see a woman cry. She swore he had never done anything like that before and she promised to make sure he didn't do it again. When I saw that the bites weren't that bad, I let her go. She did give me some money to get a new pair of jeans though. If I had shorts on it might have been much worse."

"Okay, I'm done. Only one of the bites was deep and I put some butterfly bandages on it. I cleaned them all out and put antibiotic ointment on it, but you will have to watch it to make sure you don't get an infection. Do you know if he had his rabies shots? Are you sure you shouldn't go to the doctor and have it looked at?"

"Nah, if it gets bad, I'll get it checked out. Why would I need a doctor when I have my own Florence Nightingale"? James reached over and pulled Gladys into his lap. He nuzzled her neck and then gave her a long kiss that left her gasping for breath.

Pushing him away and standing up, she straightened her hair and said, "Well, now that my nursing duties are over, I better get back to work. You sure have been having a string of bad luck. First the dent in your car and now the dog bites. Maybe I should stay away from you."

Eliott's face darkened and he glared at her, pulling away when she ruffled his hair. "Hey, I was just kidding. Don't be mad. Your luck is sure to change soon."

***

After Gladys left the room, James swallowed a couple of pain killers and went out on the pier to check on his boat.

That damn dog! I hope that bullet killed him. If not, it will at least put him out of commission for a few days. This has taken way too long to get that kid and get out of here. Gladys is a convenient cover while I am in hiding, but if I have to cuddle up to her one more time, I think I will puke. I need to end this for good.

Opening a compartment in the galley of his boat, he pulled out his new automatic pistol and checked to see if all the opiates were still in their hiding place. He cleaned the gun, looked to see that it had bullets, and wrapped it in a soft cloth before putting it away.

I have everything I came for. Its time silence the kid and get out of here.

36

Christina reached over to the small table by her porch chair and picked up the glass of Cabernet Sauvignon she had been drinking. Swirling it in the glass and watching the cathedral windows the wine formed on the sides, she sighed.

I am an accomplished doctor. I can respond quickly and efficiently in a crisis. I'm educated and old enough to make split second decisions. Why am I so confused about Brad? I get all the signals that he likes me, but he doesn't want to commit. I should just move on and concentrate on my work. But I can't! There's no doubt about how I feel. I love him. I've never met anyone who makes me feel the way he does. He makes me feel protected and at the same time, gives me the sensation that I am strong and resourceful. He respects me and doesn't dismiss me because I am a woman. When he touches me, even the most innocent touch, I get goose bumps.

I've never met a man who has so much in common with me. He is funny and laughs at even my silliest jokes. He's also sensitive. I love how close he is to his family. Someone like that would also be close to our family; if we have one together. I can see the way he hurts for his sister and her family and what they are going through right now. When he mentions Eliott James, I can feel the anger smoldering beneath his professional demeanor.

Taking a sip of the wine, Christina laid her head back on the chair and stared out at the fading sun. Suddenly, the sky was full of reds and oranges as the sunset lit up the clouds.

The winter sunsets here are absolutely beautiful. If I were a believer in omens, I would say that it portends something wonderful. The scientist in me though, knows it's just nature and has nothing to do with my personal dilemma.

Christina sighed once again as she heard the doorbell ring. *Who could that be? Maybe it is the book I ordered from Amazon?* Carrying her glass and leaving it on the kitchen counter, she headed toward the front door. Looking through the peephole she saw Brad standing there with a big bouquet of flowers.

"Come in, come in. I was just thinking of you." Christina stepped away when he leaned in for a kiss.

"Good thoughts, I hope. I've been doing nothing but thinking of you. These flowers are for you. I saw them on Alvarado Street at the Farmers Market and thought they would look beautiful in your house."

"Thank you, they are lovely. Come into the kitchen while I get a vase. Would you like a glass of wine? I have a wonderful Cab from Carmel Valley open."

"Sure, that would be great. Christina…"

"Wait just a minute while I get these flowers in water and then I can give you my whole attention." Christina arranged the red roses, golden rod, and iris in a blue glass vase. Then placed them on the dining table where they were visible from multiple rooms.

Brad poured himself a glass of wine from the open bottle and refilled Christina's glass.

"Cheers! So, what was it you were going to say?"

Brad trailed behind her as she led him out to the patio. The blazing sunset was starting to fade, but still looked amazing.

"I love this time of day. Do you hear how silent everything is? The winds have calmed down and even the birds are quiet. It's like they are also admiring nature's beauty."

"Christina" Brad took her glass and put it down, then he placed her hand in his. "I'm sorry about how I acted the last time we were together. I had some thinking to do and I needed to sort out all my feelings. With what has been going on with Bea and her family, the case, and you, my emotions have been in a whirl. You are the most wonderful woman I have ever known. When I am with you, I feel like the world is a better place. Christina, what I am trying to say, I understand we haven't known each other that long, but I think I love you. I hope you feel the same. I was stupid to doubt my feelings."

"Oh, Brad! I was just thinking about you and how much I care for you too. You are the best thing that has ever happened to me. We have been through more things in the last year than most couples have in a lifetime. Let's see wherever 'this' leads."

"That's all? You just *care* for me? I got the impression you felt like I do."

"Oh, Brad, I do. I am falling in love with you too."

Brad put his arms around her and gave her a kiss that left no question about how he felt. His questioning eyes were met with consent from hers. As the sun set, they moved slowly toward the bedroom. Brad kicked the door shut with is foot as they fell onto the bed.

37

"Boy, you look happy this morning. Did you win the lottery?"

"Can't a guy have a good day once in a while, Tom? How was your weekend?"

"Sue and I drove down the coast and had lunch at Nepenthe. Did you see the sunset last night? Even for here, that was an especially beautiful one."

"I did see it. Pretty spectacular. So, any news on the case? When you canvased the area around my sister's house, did any of the neighbors have a home security camera that might have caught something useful?"

"Remember Mrs. Collett? We talked to her before and she said she had seen someone lurking around. Well, since then she had a camera put in."

"She lives across the street, doesn't she? Did the camera show anything?"

"It sure did. We finally have a break. She had a pretty clear picture of the guy who tried to jump the fence. Like we thought, it was Eliott James!"

"Alleluia! I could kiss that old gal! Finally, some solid

information. My good mood just got a whole lot better. Good work Tom. Can you get me a copy of the video and see if you can capture a good picture of James?"

"Already done. I sent you a link to the video and the lab guys are working on the picture. I told them to send you a copy ASAP and print out copies for the squad room."

"Excellent. I better update the Chief. See you later."

***

Brad knocked on Chief Edward Murphy's door. Sticking his head in he asked, "Got a minute Chief?"

"Only if you have good news."

"I do. We finally got a break in the case of the missing girl and the attacks on my sister. One of the neighbors had a security camera and she caught a video of the man who tried to climb over my sister's fence. As we thought, it was Eliott James. Now we have proof that he is behind these attacks."

"That's great, but I won't be happy until you have him behind bars. Are there any leads on where he might be?"

"Not yet, but we are going to circulate his picture and see if anyone recognizes him."

"Okay, get to it. Talk to KSBW and see if they will

also run his picture. I'd love to have this tied up before Christmas. I don't like having a killer in our town."

"You and me both. That would be the best Christmas present ever to see his ugly mug behind bars."

38

Bea and Claire entered the office of Doctor Amanda Palumbo. There were a few toys and books on one end of the room and several stuffed chairs in front of a low coffee table. Bea admired the local seascapes on the walls. The room was empty except for the art, but Bea knew the doctor was in the room directly opposite her seat. She explained that it was important that her clients were punctual so they didn't cross paths in the waiting room. Some people were very sensitive about their privacy. *People will go to a doctor and not worry who sees them, isn't mental health just as important? We need to get over the stigma that one is crazy if they seek out help.* At exactly 2:45, the doctor opened her door to greet them.

"Hello Claire, Bea. It's so nice to see you again. I was just catching up on some paperwork. Claire, would you mind playing here for a minute while I talk to Bea? Okay? I'll see you in a minute or two. We are just in the other room. If you need us, all you have to do is knock on the door."

"Come in Bea. It's good to see you up and about again. That was a terrible accident."

"I'm coming along nicely. I still get tired, but every

day is better than the day before. When you have a child at home, there isn't a lot of time to lie around."

"That's the truth, but you need to take time to heal. I hope you are getting enough rest."

"Oh yes, Claire is a quiet little girl and seems to understand that I am still healing. Actually, she is a big help fetching things for me."

"That's great. So, how are things going with her? Is there anything I should know about?"

"She was still getting over the trauma of seeing me hit by a car and being in the hospital and then we had an intruder at the house. Our dog, Blaze, chased him off, but was shot by the man. It seems like her life is just one turmoil after another. I often come in her room in the morning and find her sleeping under her bed with the dog. It's as if she is hiding. I know she is happy with us, but she seems to know that her life is in peril. My brother has proof that it is the man who most likely killed her mother that is trying to get to her. As a possible witness to the crime, he probably wants to get to her before she starts to talk."

"That poor child. She certainly has a lot on her plate. I'll see what I can do to help her get over her anxiety. Why don't you tell her she can come in now."

***

"Hi Claire, it is so good to see you again. Do you like to blow bubbles? Have you ever done that before? No? Well, let me show you. You dip this into the soapy water and then blow. Now you try it."

Claire took the wand, dipped it and then blew quickly. Nothing happened. She tried again with the same results.

"Try blowing slow and steady and see if that helps."

Claire dipped the wand again and then blew a long, slow breath. A soapy bubble grew and grew until it floated into the air. She looked with amazement and the iridescent ball that floated across the room.

"That's it! Good job. Do some more."

As Claire blew one bubble after the other, Dr. Palumbo mentioned, as if an aside, "Sometimes, when I am feeling stressed or nervous, I like to blow out long slow breaths as if I was blowing bubbles. It helps me calm down. Maybe you can ty it too sometime."

"You know what I also like to do with bubbles? POP THEM!"

Soon, the doctor and Claire were jumping around the room trying to pop the bubbles before they popped on their own. The little girl was smiling and giggling as she blew bubbles, then rushed to catch them.

"Whew, that was fun. Let's put them away now and I have another little exercise I would like you to try. I'm going to lay out these cards that have feelings on them. See, this is the one for happy, here's sad, safe, laughing, afraid, joy, silly, loved and angry. Now, in this box there are a bunch of checkers. When I say something, I want you to put a checker on the card that tells me how you feel. You can do more than one checker on each card or more than one card, if that's how you feel. Understand? Good. Let's start, how do you feel when we blow bubbles?"

Claire put a checker on the happy card.

"What about when you play with Blaze?"

Claire put a checker on safe, and happy.

"How about when you are with Bea?

Again, Claire put checkers on safe and happy, but added one to loved.

"What about Bea's accident?"

Claire put markers on sad and angry.

"How do you feel when you think about your father?"

Claire hesitated and then put a marker on afraid and a handful on angry. Then she shoved the whole pile on the floor. She jumped up and was breathing heavily and shaking.

"Okay, Claire, when you are feeling upset, try those

long slow breaths like we did with the bubbles. That's right, in and out, in and out. Breathe in through your nose slowly and blow out in one long breath. Are you feeling better now? Great. I think that is enough for now. Why don't you go get Bea?"

"Bea, we had a very productive session today. I taught her some slow breathing that should help when she gets anxious. We also learned that she loves to blow bubbles!"

"Well, I guess we will have to add it to our shopping list. We'll see you next week at the same time. Thank you for your help."

39

B rad was pleased to see mug shots of Eliott James in the post office and several businesses around town.

His looks are pretty unusual, what with his pock marks and height. I hope one of these flyers will get us some good tips on where he is. Maybe KSBW's program will help us in the hunt. We need to get this guy locked away!

Brad drove to Salinas and down John Street, until he saw the non-descript KSBW building. Except for the multiple satellite dishes on the roof, it would be hard to know what was inside. The building was flat with brown vents covering all of the windows.

With all the crazies today, I guess they need to protect themselves from people who don't like their opinions or the way they cover the news.

Brad pulled into the parking lot behind the building and was buzzed into the reception area.

"Welcome. You must be Detective Evans. I received your phone call earlier."

"That's right. Is the editor available?"

"He isn't in right now, but you can talk to Sam Green,

he is our news anchor."

"Sure, I know Sam. He is a great newsman."

The receptionist led Brad down a hallway to Sam Green's office. Brad smiled when he saw Sam wearing his usual shorts with a suit jacket and tie. He held out his hand, "Hi Sam, it's good to see you again. I'm glad to see you didn't get all dressed up for me."

"Ha, when I'm sitting behind a desk, no one will see the shorts. If I have to wear a suit and tie, I might as well make the rest of me comfortable."

"I hear you, brother. The first thing I'll do when I retire will be to burn all my ties!"

"How can I help you, Brad?"

"We are trying to locate this man. His name is Eliott James. He has been indicated in a home invasion, attempted murder, and a possible homicide." Brad handed over the photo of James.

"Do you think you can run a clip on him? Please mentioned that he is armed and dangerous."

"I can do that. We are always willing to help the PD and get dangerous people off the streets. If it is alright with you, I'll have a camera man come in. I'll interview you about James and then we will show his photo."

"That would be great. Just warn your camera man that

my ugly mug might crack the camera!"

***

Brad sat on a stool in the film studio with a simple screen behind him. Sam Green and a camera woman were in the room with him. "Are you ready with the cameras?"

"Okay Brad, you sit here and we will have the photo of Eliott James in the background. When I point to you, begin talking. And GO!"

"I'm Detective Brad Evans with the Monterey Police Department. I would like to invoke the help of the public in finding Eliott James." The picture of James appeared on the screen behind him.

"James is wanted on a suspected homicide, attempted homicide, hit and run, and home invasion. If anyone has any information about this man, please call the number on the screen. You can leave an anonymous tip in English or Spanish. Be aware that he is armed and dangerous. I cannot stress enough that you should not approach him. Even the smallest bit of information may help us capture him."

"And, cut. Great job Brad. You are a natural."

"Maybe I'll retire early and take your job, Sam!

"Okay now, you weren't that good. I think you should stay right where you are. We'll run this on the evening and late-night news. If the Editor approves, we can also run it again in the morning. I hope you will call us with any updates on the case."

Shaking hands with Sam, Brad added, "I sure will. This is a lot of help. If anything develops you will be the first one I call. Thanks again."

***

Brad called Bea to ask if he could come over that evening.

"Of course, why don't you come over after the news? It's Taco Tuesday so I can always make a couple more."

"If you don't mind, can I come over and watch the news with you? I may be on and I want to see how they do the clip."

"Sure, that would be fine. You know you are always welcome. What is the clip about? How are you and Christina doing? Do you want to invite her too? The more the merrier."

"Thanks, I'll ask her. I spoke to KSBW today to see if they would run a clip on Eliott James to see if anyone knows where he is hiding out."

"I'm glad you told me ahead of time, we will have to make sure Claire is out of the room. I don't want her to get upset, seeing him."

***

"Pat, can you get the door? It's probably Brad and Christina."

"Hey Brad, good to see you. Where's Christina? I thought she was coming for Taco Tuesday."

"She has to work tonight. She sends her regrets. I hope Bea didn't cook too much."

"You know Bea, she always cooks too much. She still hasn't adjusted to having the boys gone. She still cooks like she is trying to fill the bottomless well of a teenage boy's appetite."

Bea came out of the kitchen, wiping her hands on an apron. Behind her, Claire was doing the same thing.

"There you are, and there is little Miss Mini Me." Brad gave Bea and Claire each a big hug.

"Thanks for having me over. Christina had to work tonight, so she couldn't make it."

"No problem, I'll wrap up a couple of tacos for you to take to her. I'm sure she will be hungry when she gets off work."

"Thanks, isn't the news about to start? Do you mind if I go in to watch? Did you have a chance to talk to Claire?"

"Yes, yes and yes. Go ahead and watch. Call me when your clip comes on."

"Claire, can you go and check on Blaze? He may need a walk in the backyard. Just be very careful with him. He is still sore from his injury."

Claire left to check on Blaze while the rest of them settled down to watch the news. The adults could see her slowly walking with limping Blaze to his spot in the back corner of the yard.

Sam Green introduced one of the other newsmen who did a report on the current water problems.

"Bea, they're going to show your famous brother after the commercials. Can you come in now?"

After the commercial they cut to the segment where Brad was asking for help locating Eliott James. The clip was very short and the news moved on to the snow up at Lake Tahoe. Pat turned off the television.

"Well Brad, you had your fifteen minutes of fame. How does it feel?"

"More like two minutes. I just hope that the news article will get us some good tips."

"Well, enough of that, let's eat. Brad, can you call Claire in from the backyard? Make sure she washes her hands."

***

Meanwhile, Gladys Jones was working at her desk in the harbormasters office when the news came on. She was not paying attention until she heard the name, Eliott James. She turned as Brad was saying, "He is armed and dangerous." Gladys raised a hand to her mouth in shock.

No, that can't be him. That picture sure looks like him though. What, he's wanted for murder? He told me it was just a domestic case. Hit and run? That would account for the damage to his car.

Gladys was reaching for a pen to write down the number to call when she felt an arm go around her neck.

"Well, what have we here? Thought you'd turn me in did you? Well, you have another think coming."

Struggling to breathe, Gladys said, "No, no, I wouldn't do that. I'm sure it must be a mistake. You wouldn't do anything like they are saying."

James tightened his hold on her neck. "Well, actually. I would do what they are saying and, unfortunately, I can't let you go free. You were a convenient place to hide, but now that is over. I'm about ready to blow this place, and you are coming with me."

James checked the harbor and then dragged her out onto his boat. He pushed her down the steps to the galley, gagged her, tied her up and threw her onto the bed.

"We are going to go for a little ride. Unfortunately for you, only one of us will be coming back."

If he had turned to look back as he headed up the stairs, he would have seen the eyes above the gag, filled with anger and not fear.

I'm not going down without a fight. I haven't lived at a harbor without meeting some pretty tough characters. It's not so easy to intimidate me. He may own a boat, but he doesn't know crap about tying knots.

Gladys relaxed her arms so that the rope had a little slack and then moved around until they started to loosen even more.

Only an amateur would tie my arms like that and in front of me. She lifted her arms and pulled the tape off her mouth. Then, with her teeth, she managed to untie the knot holding her hands together. Once her hands were free, she undid the ropes holding her feet.

Gladys quietly slid off the bed and started to explore the cabin, looking for a weapon. Opening one of the storage areas, she found his gun and the drugs. Picking up the gun and checking to see if it was loaded, she released the safety.

My, my, my, he really is a naughty boy. I wonder if there is a reward for turning him in? Otherwise, he is right; only one of us will be coming back to shore.

Gladys silently climbed to the hatch and lifted it slowly. What she had not counted on was that James had seen the hatch open up and was ready for her. As she stuck her head out of the opening, she was knocked back into the cabin by a savage blow. As she lay, confused and in pain, he came down after her. James noticed the gun on the floor.

"Oh, my goodness, it looks like you have broken your leg. How sad. I'm impressed though, I didn't think you would have the nerve to try to escape. It looks like you also found my gun. I'll take that back."

Giving her a kick in the ribs he added, "It's not going to do you much good now, is it?"

"Now, sweetheart, lets see if you can hobble up those steps again. What, it hurts? Too bad. Get up there or die now."

Gladys managed to hop up the stairs, while trying to think through the pain. What can I do now? My arms are still free. Maybe I can swim to shore or fight him off? If he is going to kill me, I'm not going to make it easy for him.

When Gladys reached the top of the stairs, she fell on the deck. She tried to kick James in the face with her good leg as he came out of the hold, but he grabbed her broken leg and gave it a twist, causing her to lose consciousness.

When she awoke, it took her a moment to orient

herself and catch her breath. Her leg was at a strange angle and her hands were, once again, tied. This time they were behind her back.

"Well, welcome back. I have to admit, you are quite the fighter. I think we are far enough at sea now to avoid any prying eyes. Is there anything you'd like to say? Final words and all that."

"Yes, you bastard. You won't get away with this."

"No last words for a loved one? No pledge of undying love? Okay then." Before she could even widen her eyes, James raised the gun and shot her in the head. Then he tied a weight to her and tossed her overboard.

I'm not going to make the mistake again of letting a body float to shore.

40

B ack at the MPD, Brad was going through a stack of papers that had accumulated on his desk. He didn't see anything that needed his immediate attention so when he noticed Tom Kent walking by, he waved him over.

"Tom, have there been any responses from the flyers or the news segment?"

"Sure, plenty, but none of them panned out. It's like Yeti, lots of sightings, but no actual proof."

"Well, we can only hope that something shakes loose soon."

"From your lips to God's ears." Tom sat on the edge of Brad's desk.

"Do you have any plans for the weekend?"

"Christina and I are going to see, 'It's a Charlie Brown Christmas', at the Wharf Theater. Do you and Sue want to come too?"

"There's a theater on the wharf? I've never seen it."

"It's down toward the end, of the wharf. I'm not surprised you never noticed it. It's a tiny little thing with only a couple of rows of seats. I saw the '***Pirates of Penzance***' there once and it was really good. You should come. We could go out to dinner at the Old Fisherman's Grotto afterwards."

"I'll ask Sue. It sounds like fun. It's strange that we live here, but we rarely go to the places that draws all the tourists. We should support the local merchants as much as the tourists do."

***

Brad, Christina, Tom and Sue were sitting in the front row of the Wharf Theater. They were so close to the actors that they could see the sweat on their brows. The other rows were filled with children and their parents.

"I'm sorry guys, I didn't realize that this production was all kids."

"I think it's cute. As soon as I heard the Charlie Brown theme song, I couldn't help but smile."

"Thanks, Christina. I was starting to feel guilty."

"Shh." Came from behind them.

Oops, it must be a parent who is here to see their child perform.

The group settled back in their chairs and were soon in the spirit of Charlie Brown and his friends trying to save

Christmas and resurrect a poor tree.

When the play finished, they walked down a short flight of stairs and were immediately on the wharf.

"Okay, that was a lot of fun after all. It wouldn't have seemed right to have adults playing the different parts."

"I agree, Sue. They were so cute, and the kid playing Snoopy was really funny."

"So true, it really got me in a good mood. After dealing with criminals all week, it was fun to see some innocent children for a change."

"We had a child this week in the ER who had been terribly injured in an accident. It was good to see healthy children singing and dancing to upbeat music."

The group walked around the chattering children who were coming out of the theater and moved a couple of doors down to the Old Fisherman's Grotto.

As they walked in, Chris Shake, the owner, was standing by the front door in his signature suit and crisp white shirt. It was impressive that he always found time to welcome his guests personally.

"Welcome, Brad. We are always happy to serve our local police. I hope you enjoy your dinner." He gave them a card for a free appetizer.

"We always do, Chris. I can't take this; I hope you understand. It might look like a bribe." Holding up his hand in a defensive position, Brad added, "I know that's not how it is meant, but someone looking on might misconstrue your actions. Let's give it to the ladies. They might want to use it. Thank you."

They were seated at a table by the windows overlooking the south side of the bay near the Coastal Trail. Even at this hour they could see walkers, bikers and couples strolling along the path.

"It's so beautiful here, when I think of the rest of the country freezing in December, I can't help but appreciate the temperate climate we have here. Look at the way the lights shine on the water, and the harbor seals sleeping on the rocks. Does it get any better than this?"

"I know what you mean, Sue. I've lived in Monterey my whole life and I never get tired of the beauty of the area. It may be expensive here, but we are really lucky to live in such a beautiful place."

When they were settled, the waiter came by. "What would you all like to drink tonight? We have a wonderful Cabernet from a local winery that you might like, but if you prefer white wine, we have a nice bottle from Scheid's."

"I think we would all like water with our dinners and, if

it alright with everyone, we would like a Gewürztraminer."
He glanced around and they all nodded in agreement.

"Good choice, I will be back in a couple of minutes
for your dinner selections."

Everyone took a few minutes looking at the menu and
discussing what they were going to order.

"Anybody know what's in season right now? I'd really
like to get something fresh."

"You can bet the food here is always fresh. Sand dabs
are always a good choice, but I think I'm going to go with a
pasta. Should we order an appetizer?"

"I would like to get a small bowl of their delicious
Clam Chowder. It has always been one of my favorites.
Anybody else?"

"That's sounds good. We could order one of their
bread bowls for the table and we could all share it."

"Great idea. In the meantime, I think I'll order the
Coconut Shrimp and the Pear Salad."

"Me too."

"You girls are light weights, I'm going for their Skirt
Steak, how about you Tom?"

"I feel like some Spaghetti and Meatballs."

Within minutes their drinks arrived and shortly thereafter the Clam Chowder.

"Boy this really is good. Lots of chunks of clams and a hint of bacon. I could eat this all by myself!"

"Save some room for your Spaghetti, Tom."

"There's always room for Spaghetti!"

At the next table was a large group of older women who were having a great time. The drinks were flowing, appetizers and meals were consumed with gusto and desserts were seen in abundance. There was a lot of laughter and you could see the deep friendship they all had with one another.

Sue asked the waiter, "What is that group over there? They are having so much fun."

"Are they bothering you?"

"On the contrary, it is wonderful to see them enjoying the evening so much."

"They call themselves 'Ocean's Eleven' because they have eleven members."

"Hmm, Ocean's Eleven, they looked younger in the movie!" Tom said with a smirk.

Trying to change the subject, Christina said, "The play was so cute. I really liked the child who played Pig Pen. He was always one of my favorites. I bet Claire would like it too. She hasn't been exposed to too many things and this play would be just right for her. Brad, you should ask if Bea or Pat can bring her before it closes."

"Speaking of Bea and Claire, did you guys get any calls after your television announcement?"

"Nothing that will help us. I just have a feeling that this case is going to bust wide open soon. He can't stay in hiding forever and when he shows himself, we will get him."

"I asked some of the homeless people to keep and eye out too. They often see things that no one else notices."

"That's probably because they aren't rushing around like everyone else. It's amazing what you notice when you sit still. Just the other day, I was sitting on my porch and saw a fox come out of the trees to sniff around the yard. I've never seen one before and I probably wouldn't have if I hadn't been sitting there quietly."

"I've lived here my whole life, Christina, and I've never seen a fox. That's so exciting. I'll have to look next time I come over."

The waiter came over with a tray of delicious looking sweets. "Anyone up for dessert?"

The question was answered by a chorus of groans. "I don't think I could eat another bite. It was all so good and your helpings were enormous.

After they asked for the check, the waiter came back with red roses for the ladies.

"That's so sweet. Thank you. I'm sure I will be back again."

"You mean you haven't been here before?"

"Like you said before, the locals somehow miss out on all the great things that the tourists seem to know. Remember, I haven't lived here as long as some of you."

Brad put his arm around Christina, "That's okay sweetie, we will forgive you." That comment earned him an elbow in the ribs.

"Oof, see Tom, don't mess with an educated woman. They always win the discussion."

Smiling, the group left the table and made their way back to their cars.

"I'll see you tomorrow, Brad. Another day, another dollar."

"I hope that you earn more than that! I'll drive mi' lady home and see you in the morning."

A few hours later, Brad was propped up on his elbow looking at Christina in the bed next to him. She was asleep and he watched her gently breathing with her hair spread out across the pillow. With her face relaxed he could picture how she must have looked as a child. She drowsily opened one eye and looked at him.

"Why are you staring at me? You should be asleep." She said groggily.

Leaning over to kiss her gently on the forehead, he answered, "I was just picturing you with pigtails and braces."

"Hmm. I don't think I ever wore braces. Go back to sleep."

Brad brushed some hair from her face and kissed her again. "Good night sweetheart." *I think I would like to stick around and also see how she looks in old age.* With that thought in mind, Brad also fell into a deep and restful sleep.

41

James rubbed the stubble on his face. *Thankfully, my beard grows fast. I can't do much about my height, but I can hide the pockmarks on my face. A hat or hoody should disguise me enough to fool most people.*

The phone rang in the Harbormaster's office and he picked it up.

"Moss Landing Harbormaster's office."

"This is Officer Tom Kent from Monterey P.D., is Ms. Jones there?"

"No, she is out for a while."

"May I ask when she will be back?"

"She said something about going down to see her daughter in Los Angeles. I'm not sure how long she will be away. I think her daughter is expecting a baby and there's Christmas coming up soon."

"May I ask who you are?"

"Oh, she just asked me to keep and eye on things until she gets back. Not much goes on here at this time of the year, so I just keep the bathrooms clean and answer the phone. If anything important happens, I just have to give her a call and she'll tell me what to do."

"Can you give me her phone number in case I have to get ahold of her?

"Sure, what are you calling about?"

Mostly I wanted to know if she has heard or seen Eliott James in the harbor. I also wanted to ask if we could put up one of our 'Wanted' posters in the office. By the way, I still didn't get your name."

"My name is, uh, Dusty Trails. I know, I know, my parents had a weird sense of humor. They were big fans of cowboy movies."

"She didn't mention anything about and Eliott James to me. Why do you think he might be here?"

"We have information that he has a boat and we were just checking with all the harbors."

"I'll ask around. You can bring down your flyer and, if the office is locked, stick it in the mailbox and I will see that it gets hung up."

"Thanks a lot Mr. Trails. I'll be down later today with a poster."

"Call me Dusty."

"Okay, Dusty, see you later."

***

After the short drive up Highway 1 to Moss Landing, Tom pulled into the lot by the Harbormaster's office. He went to the door and found it locked. He peeked in the window and didn't see anyone inside. Leaving the poster in the mail box, he saw a sign on the door to call a number if anyone needed help, so he tried to call it. He could hear it ring in the office and then an answering machine picked up.

"This is the Harbormaster, Gladys Jones. I am out of the office right now. If you need to speak with me, please leave a message with your name, your phone number and what kind of help you need and I will get back to you as soon as possible."

He tried calling Gladys' cell phone, but no one picked up.

Thinking that Dusty might be out on the docks, Tom went to look around. He went around the side of the building into the area where the showers were. He didn't see anyone inside and he was surprised at how dirty they were. *If Dusty is getting paid to keep things clean, he is sure doing a poor job of it. Well, when the cat's away, the mice do play. He'll probably do a quick clean-up when he knows she is coming back.*

Next, he went out onto the docks to see if there was a boat matching the description of James's boat that they had received previously. Since the gates to some of the docks were locked, he couldn't see very far. If he had, he would have been able to see Eliott James' boat tucked in neatly between two larger vessels.

It's strange that Dusty thought she had gone down to see her daughter who was pregnant. I'm sure she told me before that her daughter had the baby before Thanksgiving. Well, guys don't always pay attention to that stuff. Or maybe she has another pregnant daughter?

In front of the weather beaten garage he saw a white Ford Mustang and wrote down the plates. He assumed it was Gladys car, but he would check it out. If it was her car, why didn't she park in the garage? The garage was locked and there weren't any windows to peek into. *I guess that's not unusual. If she is like most people, they keep their storage in the garage and their cars in the driveway.*

42

Brad picked up the phone on his desk. "Detective Brad Evans here. Who am I speaking with?"

"Hello, Detective. This is Chief Ray Sutton, from the Monterey Coast Guard. A couple of fishermen found a body of a female and I thought you might be interested."

"Where did they find her?"

"They were fishing for some deep-water fish and their nets caught on something. When they pulled them in, they found the body. She was tied, shot and weighted down. Unfortunately, or luckily for us, the knot tying the weight came undone and she floated up."

"Where is she now?"

"After they called us, we picked her up and brought her back here to the station. I'd appreciate it if you would take her off our hands. We really don't have space to store bodies here."

"So, are you signing over jurisdiction on this?"

"Sure, but I hope you will keep us informed on what you figure out."

"Can you give me the names of the fishermen who

found her? I'd like to do some follow-up with them."

"No problem. I'll have them here for you when you pick her up."

Hanging up the phone, Brad called over to Tom Kent.

"Hey, Tom. Looks like we have another dead woman in the bay. Want to take a ride with me? They have her body over at the Coast Guard. Please notify the coroner to meet us there with his van. We need to transfer her to the morgue."

***

Brad and Tom pulled up to the Coast Guard station off of Lighthouse Avenue in Monterey. He used the intercom at the gate to announce his arrival. The coroner arrived at the same time and they all went in together. Walking up to the front desk, Brad flashed his badge and introduced himself to the young Ensign.

"I'm Detective Brad Evans from Monterey PD, this is Officer Tom Kent and Doctor Jared Parker from the Coroners Office. I received a call from Chief Ray Sutton about a body for us?"

"Yes Sir, we do. The Chief has been informed that you are here. Please take a seat. It will be just a minute or two." Before sitting, Brad and Tom walked around the lobby and looked at the pictures and memorabilia in the showcases.

Shortly thereafter, Chief Sutton came out to greet them. "Detective Evans? I'm Chief Sutton. We spoke on the phone about the body that was found in the bay."

"Yes, we did. Nice to meet you. This is Officer Tom Kent and Doctor Jared Parker from the Coroner's Office. Do you mind if we look at the body before we remove it? The less it is handled, the more chance of getting forensic evidence."

"Of course. I have a meeting in a few minutes so I hope you don't mind if my aide, Seaman Stacy Lu will continue from here. She is fully informed on the body and will be happy to answer any questions you may have."

"Of course, thank you for your time."

"Please come this way, gentlemen. As you already know, the body of a female was pulled from the bay by local fishermen. She got caught in their nets and was hauled in with their catch. I have to warn you, she is quite bloated and the birds and fish had been feeding on her."

Opening the door to a small room, the Seaman led them to a refrigerator that was being used to store the body. "We are not really equipped to handle bodies but we have this large refrigerator that isn't used very often. Luckily. We'll have to do a complete sanitation of it after this!"

"Whew, that is a nasty smell! I thought the refrigeration

would stop the deterioration."

"Unfortunately, no. The body continues to leak fluids after decomposition starts. Well, let's see what we have here."

Doctor Parker put on some gloves and unzipped the body bag. Tom began to gag and stepped outside for a minute. "I thought it was bad before! This is awful. It smells like feces and rotting flesh. I'll never get that smell out of my nose."

"Try putting a little Vaseline under your nose next time you have a body. It helps a little, although nothing will kill the smell completely."

"The body is a middle-aged, Caucasian, female. There is an obvious bullet hole in her forehead and bloating from decomposition. Damage to the eyes and exposed skin is probably due to birds and fish scavenging the body. Due to the amount of gas in the body, I would say she has been dead for twelve to twenty-four hours. I'll know more when I get her to the morgue. Liver temps agree with the twelve to twenty-four-hour window Her arms and feet are bound and you can see where she was probably weighted down with something before the knot came loose. The body is fully clothed. Jeans, flannel shirt, work boots. Long, brown hair, with the beginnings of some grey."

Tom entered the room again just as Brad said, "Wait, I think I know her. Isn't that the Harbormaster from Moss Landing? What was her name, Tom?"

"Gladys Jones. Yes, I think that's her. Without the eyes and the bloating, it's hard to say for sure, but I'd bet the ranch that it's her. No wonder she wasn't at work. She was dead."

"That's tough, she was a nice lady. I think we will have to go back out and talk to this Dusty Trails again."

The Seaman, who had been standing by the back wall with her arms crossed, stepped forward. "I thought that's who it was, but I didn't want to say anything that might sway your investigation."

Doc Parker asked, "Who's Dusty Trails? What a weird name."

"It's the guy who is supposedly watching the shop while Gladys was away."

Doc Parker finished making some notes and then zipped the bag shut again. A couple of other Seamen were called to help him load her into the van. In the meantime, Brad went with the Seaman Lu to sign a transfer paper.

"Thanks for your help with this, it can't be pleasant for you."

"Unfortunately, that is one of the worst parts of the job. Recovering bodies is always hard and especially when they are the victims of a crime. I hope you find who did this. Through my work in the bay I have had some interactions with Gladys and she was always a strong and capable person."

"We'll do our best. Didn't you say the fishermen who found her would be here to answer some questions?"

"Yes sir, they are. They are in the mess hall having some coffee. I'll take you there."

***

As the men entered the eating area, they could see two men sitting at one of the tables, quietly talking while they sipped from a couple of cups.

"Hello, I'm Detective Brad Evans and this is Officer Tom Kent. Thank you for waiting. We wanted to ask you a couple of questions and then you can get back to work."

Brad pulled out a little notebook and pencil. "What are your names?"

"He's Benny Conigiloni, and I'm Tomas Aeiolli"

"Where did you find the body?"

"We were out in the Bay about fifteen miles out, fishing for rock cod. When we pulled in our nets and poured the catch into the hold, we saw her body." Looking at his friend he said, "It was really a shock. She was tied up and so nasty looking. She was all bloated and had seaweed in her hair." Gagging a little he added, "Her eyes were gone and there was a hole in her forehead. Right, Benny?"

'Yeah, sure was. I ain't never seen anything like it. I seen plenty of dead fish, but never a dead woman." Benny crossed himself. "As soon as we had our load secured, we called the Coast Guard and they came out and got her."

"Did you touch the body?"

"Naw, we pulled her out of the hold and laid her on the deck until the Guard came. We didn't even cut off the ropes. I seen enough cop shows to know you don't mess with a body."

"Okay, thanks, what time was this?"

"Early, nineish? Is that about right? We didn't look at the clock, but we'd been out a couple of hours already."

"Yeah, it was around nine."

Looking at his notebook, Brad asked, "Do you have anything else to add? Tom will get your addresses and contact information, but if you think of anything else, please give me a call. Here is my card."

43

"Tom. I think it's time we did another visit to Moss Landing. I need to follow up with this Dusty Trails guy to see what he knows about all of this."

"Okay, I'm on it. Do you want to go together or should I check him out myself?"

"I have some paperwork on Gladys Jones to finish here, so it would help if you go and talk to him. Call ahead to let him know you are coming. It won't do any good to drive all the way out there, just to miss him again. I want to know when he saw her last."

***

"Mister Trails, I mean Dusty, this is Officer Kent from Monterey again. I was wondering if I could come over and talk to you? Just some follow-up questions about Gladys. I can be there in about a half hour. Would that be okay? Alright, see you then."

The short drive from Monterey to Moss Landing was beautiful. Winding along Highway One between sand dunes and artichoke or strawberry fields, Tom found it enjoyable to get out of Monterey for a while. Between the dunes he could see glimpses of the Monterey Bay and pelicans skimming along the tops of the waves.

Most people moved over when they saw a police vehicle, but there were also the ones who slowed down, to ridiculously slow speeds when they saw him in their rear-view mirrors. *It's good, I'm not highway patrol, or I'd give some of these guys tickets for going too slow! After I see Dusty, I think I'll stop at Phil's and pick up an order of cioppino for dinner. Maybe Sue will join me.*

Tom made a quick call to Doctor Susan Blake and left a voice mail inviting her to come over for dinner around six. He spent the rest of the drive day-dreaming about her.

Tom could see the two five hundred foot towers of the power plant in Moss Landing. Even though they weren't used anymore, they were a landmark for the town. Pulling into the harbor, Tom parked his car and walked toward the Harbormasters office. He noticed that the flyer he had left was not on display in the window. Looking inside, he saw a man behind the front desk. He had a full beard, sunglasses and a hat on his head. It was hard to tell his height because he was sitting down behind the counter. Tom knocked on the window and the man waved him in.

"Hello, you must be Dusty Trails. It's good to finally put a face to the voice on the phone. I'm Officer Tom Kent from Monterey." Tom held out his ID for Dusty to see.

Dusty barely glanced at it as he sat in the swivel chair behind the counter.

"What can I do for you, Officer? There isn't much more I can tell you than I did before."

"I noticed you didn't put up the flyer I left you. "

"Oh, I'm sorry about that. I guess it got shuffled under some of the other paperwork in the office. Have you caught the guy yet?"

"No, we haven't. That's why it is important to get the word out. But, that's not why I came by. I wanted to ask when you last saw Gladys. Are you sure she was going down to Los Angeles to see her daughter?"

"Well, that's what she told me. I think it was about four or five days ago when she left."

"Is that her car in front of the garage?"

"Yeah, I drove her over to the airport in Monterey so she could leave her car here instead of long-term parking."

"When I spoke to Gladys before, she said her daughter had given birth to a baby around Thanksgiving." Flipping through his notebook, Tom added, "But you said she was going down there because her daughter was due to give birth. Is that true?"

Scratching his head, James, aka Dusty, said, "I might have said that. Honestly, when women start talking about babies, I sort of tune out."

"You haven't heard from her since she left?"

"Nope, it's been running smooth here so there wasn't any reason to call her and she hasn't checked in."

"Well, Dusty. I hate to tell you that she hasn't checked in because she is dead. Her body was found in the bay by some fishermen. She was shot in the head. Would you know anything about that?"

Tom was watching Dusty's face for his reaction. There was surprise, but not what he would have expected from someone who was just told his friend had been murdered and tossed in the bay. There was just something about him and his answers that didn't sit well with Tom. Now this lack of emotion about his friend's death set off alarm bells for him.

"Oh man, that's tough. I just saw her a little while ago. I thought she was in LA having a good time with her daughter."

"Why don't you come with me to the PD to answer some questions? I think you might be able to help us find her killer."

"Can't you ask me now? Why do I have to go to the police department? Did I do something wrong?"

"No, not at all. I'm just the boots on the street.

The detective handling her case will want to ask you a few questions. Not a big thing. We'll bring you back afterwards."

"In that case, okay. Anything I can do to help."

Just then, Tom's cell phone rang. He took it out and saw that it was Brad on the other end. He turned his back to Dusty and answered the phone. "Hey Brad. Yeah, I'm, at the Harbormasters office in Moss Landing. I'm going to bring in Dusty Trails to see if he can answer some questions for you. Sure, I'll look for the boat first. No problem."

As Tom turned back around, he fleetingly saw something out of the corner of his eye. Before he could react, he received a strong blow to the head. It knocked him off his feet and left him unconscious. Eliott James locked the door and dragged Tom into the back room. Using Tom's own handcuffs, he sat Tom on the floor and locked his hands over his head and around a pipe on the wall. Next, he tied his feet together with a plastic handcuff and then tied that with a rope to a heavy, oak, table on the other side of the room. This stretched his legs out straight so he couldn't bend them. Finally, he stuffed a rag in Tom's mouth and tied another around his face to keep him from spitting the gag out.

That should hold him for a while. If he struggles, the

knot will just get tighter. I don't think anyone will find him here. In the meantime, I'm going to grab the kid and get out of here. I can't believe that Gladys was found already. What dumb luck.

44

Brad glanced at his watch. *I wonder where Tom is? He said he would be bringing Dusty Trails in to answer some questions. I'll give him a call and see what's holding him up.*

Brad called Tom's cell phone. It rang at least ten times and no one answered. Next, he called the dispatcher. "Hi Jocelyn, can you give a call out to Tom Kent's patrol car and see where he is? Tell him I am waiting for him at MPD. Thanks."

"Sure thing, Detective. I can see on his GPS that his car is in Moss Landing."

"Moss Landing? He should have left there hours ago. Tell me if you reach him."

A few minutes later, Jocelyn called back. "There isn't any response from his car and it hasn't moved."

"Thanks. I better see what's going on."

Brad grabbed his car keys and headed out to the parking lot behind the building. He stopped by the Chief Murphy's office. He knocked on the window and the Chief waved him in.

"What's up, Brad?"

"Chief, I'm worried about Tom Kent. I sent him out to Moss Landing to talk to the Harbormaster about Gladys Jones and he hasn't returned. His phone doesn't pick up and neither does the radio in his patrol car. Dispatch says the car is still parked in Moss Landing. I have a bad feeling that he is in trouble. Can I take another uniform with me to check it out?"

"Sure. Tom's a good cop and it isn't like him to not check in. Keep me informed."

"Will do, Chief."

Brad strode through the bull pen and grabbed one of the senior officers. When he told him why he needed back-up, the officer grabbed his gun and led Brad to his squad car.

On the way to Moss Landing, Brad filled him in on why he was worried. They worked out a plan where they would park around the corner and then walk carefully to the office. Brad went toward the front of the building. He saw Tom's car and looked in the windows to be sure he wasn't inside. He motioned the police officer to the other side of the door of the Harbormaster's office and quickly ran up in a crouch. Peeking quickly, in the window, he couldn't see anyone inside. He tried the door and it was locked. Nodding to the officer, he kicked in the door and they entered with their guns drawn.

"Police! Is anyone in here? Come out with your hands up!"

They quickly ran behind the counter. Brad noticed some blood on the ground and silently pointed it out to the other man. They went toward the back room and once again gave a warning.

"Monterey Police! We are coming in. Put down your weapons and put up your hands."

Upon entering the room, they saw Tom slumped near the wall with blood on his head. They cleared the room and went to him. Brad felt for a pulse while the officer released his handcuffs and untied his legs while Brad tried to talk to him.

"He has a pulse. Tom, Tom, can you hear me? Tom? He's not responding."

Brad dialed the dispatcher. "Jocelyn, this is Brad Evans. I'm at the Moss Landing Harbormasters office. Tom is here with a head wound. He is unresponsive. Can you send an ambulance right away? Thanks."

Next, he dialed the Chief. "Chief, this is Brad. I found Tom. He has been knocked out. Jocelyn has an ambulance on the way, but we will need a forensics team here to see if we can get any clue to what happened. Uh huh, Tom is out cold. He won't be telling us anything for a while. It looks like he was hit in the temple. Say a prayer that he will be alright."

The Officer had secured the scene and stood at the door to make sure no one else came in. Within fifteen minutes, the forensics team was there, as well as the ambulance. They checked on Tom's vital signs and loaded him in the ambulance.

"Where are you taking him?"

"Salinas Valley. It is a trauma center and can do more to help this kind of emergency. Don't worry, his vital signs are good and we will make sure he gets the best care possible."

Brad turned to the forensics team. "Hey Doc, thanks for coming so quickly."

"Of course, this is one of our own. We will nail whomever did this."

"I think I have a pretty good idea. Tom came out here to check if the temporary Harbormaster knew anything about Gladys Jones death. The next thing we know, Tom is missing and we find him knocked out. I would bet my last dollar that it was Eliott James who did this."

"It's possible, but let's let the facts and evidence convict him...not just hunches." The doctor put his hand on Brad's shoulder. "I know it must be hard to see him like this, especially after you lost another officer last year."

"Yeah, it really is, but I'm not going to lose Tom, if I can help it. I think I will call Dr. Susan Blake and tell her what happened. They are close and she would want to know. She might also be able to get some information that we can't."

Tom walked away and dialed Sue's number. "Hi Sue, it's Brad."

"Hi Brad. What's up? How can I help you?"

"I'm afraid I have some bad news. Tom was attacked today. He has a bad head wound and is unconscious. They've taken him to Salinas Valley Hospital. I thought you would want to know."

There was a moment of dead air on the phone. "Thanks Brad. I do want to know. I will get over there as soon as I can get away from here. Luckily, its quiet and my shift is almost over. I'll tell Christina, if that's okay."

"Sure. We are all friends and she would want to know. Are you okay?"

"I think so. It's a shock, but we have talked about how he has a dangerous job. I just never thought anything would really happen. You know what I mean? I've got to go, but I should be able to be there in a half hour or so."

"Great. I'll see you there when I finish up here."

45

Brad was pacing in the hallway outside of the ER. A doctor came out of the room that Tom was in and approached Brad.

"Hello, I'm Doctor Malcolm Roberts. Your officer suffered a severe blow to the right temple. We did a CT scan and he has blood draining into his skull. Right now, he is unconscious. We hope that will change after we release the pressure on his brain. We are taking him into surgery to drain the blood. It is a very serious problem, but we are hopeful that you found him in time before there was too much damage to the brain. The neurological surgeon we have is excellent and will do all he can to help him."

"Thank you, doctor. I'll wait for him to come out of surgery, if that's okay."

"Of course, I'll have a volunteer take you to the waiting room. Try not to worry. He is in good hands."

"By the way, his girlfriend is a doctor at CHOMP. She will probably want to be updated on his condition."

"That's fine. Have her check in when she gets here."

While Brad was talking to the ER doctor, his brothers

in blue had started to arrive at the hospital. While they knew that they had dangerous jobs, they also knew that danger created a bond that few others would have. No one would ever be left behind or left alone in times of peril. They were milling around, talking quietly in small groups. Some were in uniform and many were in street clothes and had come in from home. When Chief Murphy arrived, Brad went over to fill him in on Tom's condition.

"Hi Chief, thank you for coming to add support."

"Of course. Tom is one of our family and we don't let family suffer alone."

"I just spoke with the doctor. Tom received a blow to the head and has bleeding on the brain. They are going to do surgery to relieve the pressure."

"Thanks, Brad." Turning toward the assembled officers, Chief Murphy called for attention. "Thank you all for being here. As you know, Tom was injured in the line of duty. He had a severe blow to the head and has a brain bleed. They are going to perform surgery to drain the blood and reduce the pressure on his brain. He is young and he is tough, but this is a very dangerous surgery. If you are the praying kind, keep him in your prayers and ask that god is with him and his surgeons. I see that Father Mike is here. Father, can you say a prayer for Tom?"

"Of course, Chief." Please bow your heads. The bustling room quieted as one officer after another bowed his head and removed their hat. "Dear Heavenly Father. We know that you love your children and want only good things for them. Your son healed Lazarus and brought him back from death. We pray that, in your holy mercy, you will bring our friend and comrade, Tom Kent, back from this terrible injury. Be with the surgeons and guide their hands. Be with us as we mourn for his injury. In the name of your son, Jesus, we ask this. Amen."

A chorus of Amens resounded in the room and more than one officer was seen to wipe a tear from his or her eye. When Brad lifted his head, he saw Sue and Christina enter the room. He hurried over to them and gave them each a hug.

"Hi, did you hear the Chief explain what happened?"

"No, we didn't. Can you fill us in?"

"Tom received a blow to the head and has bleeding on the brain. They are going to do a surgery to drain the blood and release the pressure. Sue, I told them you were coming and would like to be kept in the loop."

"I don't have privileges at this hospital, but I hope, professional courtesy will allow me to get a more detailed report. Can you tell me who you spoke to?"

"It was Doctor Malcolm Roberts. He saw Tom in the ER, but is not doing the surgery. They have a neurosurgeon doing that."

Christina had been holding Sue's hand but she released it and gave her a hug as Sue went to find Doctor Roberts.

"How is she doing, Christina?"

"As well as can be expected. As a doctor, she knows he will have the best care possible, but she also knows all the things that could go wrong. She's scared, as we all are, but her relationship is much closer than ours, so she feels it more intensely. I am amazed at all the people who are here."

"Except for the guys who are working the scene of the crime, everyone who can is here. We support our own."

"Has anyone called his parents?"

"Not yet. I'll call Jocelyn at Dispatch and have her get me their number from his file. They've already lost one son to violence; they will be heartbroken to hear he has been injured."

"Here comes Sue, maybe she has their number."

"Hi Sue, did you get a hold of Doctor Roberts?"

"Yes, he filled me in on what's happening. Tom is going to have a burr hole drilled in his skull to allow them to drain the hematoma. Luckily, it seems to be localized. It is much better than a craniotomy, but still has risks. He will have to be watched for infection and more bleeding. His recovery is going to be long and possibly, not complete. The first three months will tell us more. Right now, he just has to make it through the surgery."

"Wow, that sounds terrible. You know we are here for him and you. Sue, do you have the phone number for Tom's parents? I think they will want to know."

"I do have the number. Would you mind calling them? If I have to face them, I might lose it. Right now, I am just hanging on by a thread."

"Of course I can. He was there because I asked him to be. I feel responsible. If I had gone there when I said I would, maybe this wouldn't have happened."

Christina put her hand on his arm. "Brad, you have nothing to feel responsible for. You were doing your job and so was he. The only one responsible is the one who did this."

Brad took the number from Sue and walked into a quiet corner of the hallway to make the call. Christina could tell from his tense posture that it was hard for him. At one point, he straightened up from the waist as if receiving a blow. He spoke a few words and hung up with a sigh.

Brad rubbed the back of his neck. "That was tough. His mother answered the phone and just started moaning after I told her he was in the hospital. Tom's dad took the phone from her and I had to tell him all over again. You could hear the pain and concern in his voice, but he was able to keep his emotions in control. They will get the first flight here that they can. They live in Washington state, so it isn't too far away. I asked if they need a place to stay and they told me that Tom had an extra bedroom at his place."

"Sue, did you have any trouble talking to the doctor? Not at all, besides being a doctor, which would have been enough, I told him we were engaged."

"What? Is that true?"

Sue lifted her hand and showed Christina the diamond ring on her finger. "We got engaged on the weekend. I know it is fast but we are both sure of our feelings. We haven't had time to tell anyone yet. It was supposed to be a surprise."

"Congratulations! That's great. I've had time to get to know him pretty well on the job and he is a great guy. You are both very lucky to have found each other."

"I agree. I have to thank Christina for bringing me along on Thanksgiving. It seems so long ago, but it has only been a few weeks."

"Speaking of which, are you sure you aren't rushing

things? I don't want to be Debby Downer, but I also don't want either of you to get hurt."

"We are sure. We are old enough to know what we want and we are in sync on so many things, that we couldn't believe it. I didn't used to believe in love at first sight, but since I met Tom, I know it can happen. He feels the same way."

Christina gave Sue a hug. "Well, he is lucky to have you. Have you set a date yet?"

"No, not yet. With his injury, I think it will be a long time before he is able to plan anything. Let's see how his recovery goes first."

46

Sue went to check on the status of Tom's operation while the rest of his friends and the other officers milled around waiting for news. It was a couple of hours since he went in to the operating room, but no one had left. They all wanted to be there for Tom. Christina had fallen asleep in one of the chairs with her head on Brad's shoulder. Other police officers were standing in the hall talking quietly or drinking cups of coffee. The overall mood was somber and tense. Each of the men and women who wore the uniform of the Monterey PD, knew that their job was dangerous and they put their lives on the line every day. There was the disquieting thought; *that could be me next.* "I've got your back," was not something they said idly. Through thick and thin they would stand by their brothers in blue.

The door to the waiting room opened and Sue walked in with Doctor Roberts. The room immediately grew silent as they all turned toward the two doctors. Those who were sitting, slowly stood up. "I have some good and some bad news. Tom's surgery went very well. We were able to relieve the pressure on his brain and stop the bleeding." An audible sigh of relief went around the room and everyone began to smile. "But…the bad news is that we do not know how much damage was done. Even with minimal damage, it will be a long recovery. He will have headaches, and need extensive physical therapy to get back to normal. There is always the chance that he may not regain all the capabilities he had before the injury. Doctor Blake can answer any other questions you have."

Brad stood up with Christina at his side and shook Doctor Robert's hand. "Thank you so much for what you did. We will do all we can to help him with his recovery. I'm sure all the other people here feel the same."

Sue answered a few questions and then addressed the group. "Tom is sleeping now and will be out for quite a while. You can all go home now and we will call the station if anything changes. In a couple of days, you should be able to visit him, but keep it really short and only one or two people at a time. Thank you all for coming. If he could see your support, it would definitely raise his spirits. He isn't out of the woods yet, and your continued presence and prayers are needed and appreciated."

As the officers slowly turned to leave, it was like they took the heavy atmosphere with them. Now the air was filled with hope and determination.

Chief Murphy came over to talk to Brad. "I better get

back to work. Are you going to stay? You can take all the time you want. I know you have grown close to Tom."

"I'd like to stay for a while, but then I am going to get back to work. I want to catch the guy who did this and bring him to justice."

"Just don't let your emotions get in the way. Make sure you follow the letter of the law and do everything right. We don't want him to be released later by the courts because of some small slip up."

"Don't worry about that. When I catch this guy, he will stay caught."

***

Sue was sitting next to Tom's bed in the ICU. He was very pale and his head was wrapped in bandages. There was an IV line in his arm and leads from the heart monitor leading to his chest. A blood pressure cuff was on his arm and inflated every so often. An oxygen line was looped over his ears and attached to his nostrils. She glanced at the monitor and saw that his heartbeat and pulse were in the normal range, as was his, blood pressure. When she glanced back at the bed, she could see his eyes looking at her questioning.

Sue reached over to hold his hand and gave it a squeeze. "Welcome back. Do you remember anything that happened? Do you know where you are?" Tom shook his head no and then grimaced from the pain it caused.

Sue held a cup with a straw to his mouth and gave him a small sip of water. "Brad found you in the Harbormaster's office in Moss Landing. You were unconscious with a severe head injury. You were rushed to Salinas Valley Memorial Hospital and you had surgery to relieve the pressure on your brain. The surgery was successful and you have been sedated for two days. You are still in the ICU. Do you remember any of this?" Again, he painfully shook his head. "Do you remember me?" He smiled at her and Sue let out a breath that she didn't realize she had been holding in.

"All the officers from your station were here, even the Chief. Brad has been here around the clock and Christina, Bea and Pat have all stopped in to see you. Everyone has been praying for you and stopping in to give encouragement. You are a lucky man to have so many people who care about you." Sue realized that Tom had already drifted back to sleep so she stepped out to inform the nurses that he had been awake. Then she went out to find a very ragged and scruffy, Brad.

"Hi Brad, I just wanted to tell you that Tom woke up for a couple of minutes. I told him what had happened but he doesn't remember anything. His memory may, or may not, come back as he heals."

"Did he tell you anything?"

"No, he just nodded his head when I asked him questions. He hasn't said anything yet. But he did recognize me, which is a very good sign. I better get back. I think you should go home and get some rest, food and a shower. I will be here if anything changes."

Rubbing the beard on his face, Brad agreed that he could use some sleep and a shower, but promised to return as soon as he could. He gave Sue a hug and asked how she was doing.

"I'm as good as can be expected. It is very hard to see someone you love so injured and in pain. At least, as a doctor, they are keeping me updated on his progress. I've been able to go home a couple of times when his parents came by. They are just as sweet as he is. They have welcomed me with loving arms. It's sad to say, but I think his injury has brought us closer together than it would have happened normally. They were surprised, but excited that we were engaged. Oh, here they are now. Let me update them on Tom and then I will walk out with you."

Tom's parent's talked to Sue for a couple of minutes and then walked over to Brad. Tom's father stretched out his hand and shook Brad's with vigor. "Thank you so much for being here for our son. He has spoken so highly of you that I feel like I already know you."

"It's my pleasure. Tom is a wonderful man; I wish we could clone him. I'll be here for him as long as he needs me. The whole station is here for him. He is very well respected in the department. I'm going home to catch a nap and clean up a little, but I will be back later."

"Don't worry. We will be here when you get back. Both you and Sue have done more than we could ever expect."

47

Bea and Claire were in the back of the house watching Blaze chasing a squirrel around the backyard. Seeing a worried look on Claire's face, Bea said, "Don't worry Claire. Blaze is not going to hurt the squirrel. He is too fast for the dog and he will jump into a tree to get away. It is more of a game for the two of them. Both of them know that Blaze doesn't have a chance to catch the squirrel. Look, he is already in the tree." Blaze sat down and looked longingly at the squirrel. "I think he is waiting to see if it will come down again. A big dog like that needs lots of exercise and chasing squirrels will do that for him!"

The front doorbell rang and Claire ran off to answer the door. Flinging open the door, Claire stepped back in horror as she saw her father in the opening. He stepped inside after her and grabbed her by the arm. As he started to pull the struggling child outside, Bea came around the corner. "Claire, don't open the door until I get there…". Her voice trailed off when she saw a man with his arm around Claire.

"Who are you? What do you want?"

"I want my kid back. You have no right to keep her from her father."

Seeing the look of fear on Claire's face, Bea asked, "Claire, is this your father? Do you want to go with him?"

Claire nodded her head and twisted to get out of his arms. "You put her down, right now! She doesn't want to go with you. You can ask the courts to straighten this out."

"The courts? That's a laugh. What are you going to do about it? You can't stop me and I don't see that ugly dog of yours either."

Stepping further into the room, James shut the door behind him and said, "If you don't want her to get hurt, you will do what I say. Go sit down at the table." He ripped a curtain tieback from the wall by the window and closed the shades.

"Stop wiggling, you brat." He slapped Claire across the face, temporarily stunning her.

This infuriated Bea and she rushed toward him like a mother bear protecting her young. "YOU LEAVE HER ALONE!"

James shoved Claire to the side and took a swing at Bea. She ducked and the blow went flying by her head. As she straightened up, she was hit in the side of the head by another blow. It knocked her down and temporarily stunned her, but she reached out and felt the cane she had been using, withing reach. Claire had rushed to her side when she saw

Bea get hit.

"Stand behind me darling. I will protect you or die trying." Bea stood up and raised the cane taking and a vicious swing at James. He blocked the blow with his forearm and grabbed the cane. He twisted it out of her hand and hit her again on the side of the head. She crumpled to the ground, but this time she did not get up.

Claire was shaking her and pulling on her arm, trying to get her to rise, when James grabbed her again. "Sit here or you will get the same thing."

Claire was sobbing, but sat in the chair while James tied Bea's hands and feet with the curtain cords. Grabbing the child by the arm, he dragged her toward the door again, giving Bea a kick as he walked by. "Serves you right. No woman can stop me. Her mother couldn't and neither can you."

Claire tried, once again, to break away so, James grabbed her hair and her red ribbon fell to the ground. James dragged her out of the house. He took her to the car and threw her in the passenger seat. She tried to get out when he walked around the other side of the car. James ran back and gave her a vicious slap that knocked her sideways. "Get in the car and stay there!" James growled.

He slammed the car door and ran around to the driver's

side. He got in, without looking, he backed out, and took off with the tires squealing. What he didn't see was Mrs. Collett peeking out from behind her curtains and writing down his license plate number.

Once he was out of sight, she ran out of her house, across the front yard and into the street. She ran up the Oakley's front steps and stopped at the front door. The door was open, so she peeked around the corner. "Hello, anyone home? Bea, are you there?" Once she stepped all the way into the room, she saw Bea lying on the ground. Mrs. Collett ran to her and kneeled down. "Bea, are you okay? Bea, can you hear me?"

Bea groaned and tried to rise, but couldn't because of the restraints.

Mrs. Collett untied Bea's legs and arms. "Just rest there a minute. I'm going to all 911."

Bea moaned, "Claire. He has Claire."

"We'll get her back. Don't worry. You rest now while I call for help."

"My neighbor has been attacked. I found her laying on the ground moaning. It looks like she has had a blow to the head and a large cut on her head."

"We will send an ambulance to the address on the phone you are calling from. Don't hang up until they get there."

"I won't. Can you please call Detective Brad Evans at the Monterey Police Department? The victim is his sister. I also saw Bea's little girl being dragged away by a strange man."

"I will do that right away. Please stay there. I'm sure they will have questions for you."

48

Within minutes, Mrs. Collett could hear the sirens from the ambulance and the distinctive siren of a police vehicle. When they pulled up into the driveway, she told the operator that the rescue squad was there and hung up. She called out to them as they entered the house.

"I'm so glad you are here. Her name is Bea Oakley and she is breathing, but has a head injury."

"Thank you, mam. Please step back and let us do our work."

Mrs. Collett stepped back into the dining room watched as they put a neck splint around her neck and gently turned her onto her back. The EMT's lifted her eyelids, checked her blood pressure and pulse and put an IV in her arm. They pressed a pad to the wound on her head to stop the bleeding. The men and women were precise and efficient as they worked on her.

While two of the EMT's were working on Bea, a young man came over and asked for her name and contact information.

"It looks like she has a large wound on her head and a

bump. Did you see how it happened? Was it an accident?"

"No, this was no accident. I found her like this when I came over, but I had seen a big man dragging her little girl out of the house and hitting her really hard, before shoving her into the car. I'm pretty sure he did this to Bea too."

Brad came into the room as they were lifting her onto a stretcher. "Wait, what happened? Where are you taking her?"

"Her neighbor found her. It looks like she was hit on the head. We are taking her to CHOMP to stitch up the wound and evaluate her for concussion."

"I'll call her husband to meet you there. She just recently had another head injury. CHOMP should have all the records."

Bea reached out her hand from the stretcher. "Brad, I tried to stop him. He took Claire. Poor child. Don't worry about me. Get her back. Please, save her before he does something terrible to her."

"You just take care of yourself. I'll move heaven and earth to get her back."

"I'm sorry sir, we have to get her into the ambulance."

"Of course, of course." Giving Bea's hand a pat and kissing her on the forehead, Brad let the EMT's take her to the ambulance.

Brad called Pat Oakley to tell him what had happened and then called Christina to ask her to check in and make sure she was getting good care.

"Oh Brad, I am so sorry. Of course, I will check on her, but any doctor here would give her great care. Are you coming over too?"

"I have to interview the witness and follow up on what happened. I'll get there as soon as I can. Gotta go. Love you."

Mrs. Collett approached Brad. "I am so sorry this happened. Your sister is a beautiful person. I hope she will be okay."

"Thank you. Why are you here? Did you see what happened?"

"I was looking out my window and saw that tall man you have been looking for, dragging that poor little girl out of the house. He hit her and threw her into his car. I didn't see Bea, so I went over to see if she knew what was going on. The front door was open and I found her lying on the ground. She was moaning and asked where Claire was. She had an obvious wound on her head so I immediately called 911."

"Thank you so much. I hate to think she would have lain there until Pat came home from work. Are you sure it was the same man?"

"I may be old, but I'm not senile. It was the same one. Tall with pock marks on his face."

"What kind of car was he driving?"

"I don't know much about cars. About all I can say was it was white and had a running horse logo on the front grill. I'll do you one better, though; I wrote down the license plate number. Here it is."

"Taking the number from Mrs. Collett, Brad said, "Mrs. Collett, I could kiss you."

She blushed. "Well, what's stopping you?"

Brad leaned down and gave the little woman a kiss on the cheek, sending her into a fit of giggling.

Handing the number to one of the uniformed police officers he said, "Put a bolo out on this number. I want to know immediately if anyone sees him."

49

Claire cowered in the corner near the door of the speeding car. Her shoulders hunched around her ears and her knees were drawn up to her chest. Her tear-filled eyes glanced at James, but quickly darted away.

"Happy to see me, brat? I figured they would be so busy taking care of the cop I hit at the Harbormasters house that they wouldn't be watching the house you were in. As usual, I was right. By the time they find Bea and figure out who took you, we will be long gone on the boat. It's time I got out of this town. It is getting to hot for me to be safe anymore. You better be a good little girl or I will toss you out of the car. At this speed, it would be deadly."

Claire didn't change her position, but she grabbed onto the door handle to keep herself from flying around the car as James raced down the road. She was filled with a feeling of despair and loss. She had just begun to feel safe and loved with Bea and Pat. Now, that was all over.

"I don't like you! I don't want to go with you! I want to go back to Bea and Pat."

Reaching over to give her another slap, the car began

to weave back and forth on the road. Sitting back up and straightening the car, James said, "Well kid, I don't like you much either. I thought you couldn't talk. Looks like you found your voice. All the more reason to get rid of you. I can't have you telling everyone what I did to your mother. I wanted her to get rid of you the minute you were born, but she wouldn't do it. Well, she isn't here to stop me anymore. I really didn't mean to kill her, but it would have happened eventually. I was getting tired of her."

Holding a hand to her stinging cheek, Claire said, "Uncle Brad will get you. He won't let you hurt me."

James faked a lunge toward the girl and laughed when she cringed. "You can wish all you want, but he isn't going to save you this time. He doesn't even know you are gone."

50

The ambulance pulled up to the Community Hospital of Monterey and the driver jumped out and ran around to the back to open the doors. He helped the other paramedics move her stretcher out of the van and onto the ramp leading into the emergency room. As the legs on the gurney dropped down, Bea grimaced in pain. She would have grabbed her head if she hadn't been hooked up to so many lines.

"Can't you give me something for the pain?"

"I'm sorry, we can't give you anything until we know if you have a brain bleed. Anything with aspirin in it would just make you bleed more."

"There must be something you can do?"

"We are here now and the doctors will take care of you. We are trying to make you as comfortable as possible."

They rushed her into the emergency room and were surrounded by nurses and the doctor on duty.

"We have a white female, forty-nine years old, 190 pounds. A blow to the side of the head and a laceration on her scalp. She is awake and responsive, but complaining of head pain. Her name is Bea Oakley. She should be in your system from a recent car accident."

"Thanks, guys. We'll take it from here."

"Hey Bea. I didn't expect to see you back here so soon. So, you hit your head?"

"More like, I was hit in the head. Someone came to kidnap my daughter and when I tried to stop him, he hit me on the head and tied me up." Struggling to get off the gurney, Bea added, "Give me something for this headache and I'll be going."

Putting a hand on her arm, the nurse said, "Wait up there. We need to check you out first. We don't want you running out of here with a traumatic brain injury. Hang in there while we check your brain and stitch up the cut on your head. The doctor will be here in a minute and I'll clean the wound while we wait."

"Can you at least call my husband and tell him I will need a ride home? His number is on my chart as my contact person."

Turning to another nurse, the senior nurse said, "Go call her husband while I clean her up. We don't know yet when she will be released, but he should be notified."

***

The doctor came in and looked at her chart. "Well, Mrs. Oakley, I see you have a little bump on the head."

"Please call me Bea. I am a friend of Dr. Christina Vlk. Is she here? She can take care of me."

"She is a fine doctor, but she isn't here right now, so I guess you are stuck with me. I am Doctor Holiday. I know, I know, please no jokes about Doc Holiday and the OK Corral. I've heard them all."

"The wound on your head is minor. I think we can patch it up with some glue and a few steri-strips. Can you follow my finger while just using your eyes? Good. Do you have any blurry vision? No? Good. Dizziness? Do you feel like you are going to faint? Did you lose consciousness? No? Pupils are even and tracking. Now, let's see you stand up and check your balance. Can you take a couple of steps?"

Bea wobbled and had to reach out and grab the arm of the doctor next to her.

"A little shaky balance is to be expected, but not too concerning." Sitting her back on the bed, he asked, "Do you have any ringing in your ears? Sensitivity to light? I want you to remember these three words; car, plate, banana. I'm going to take a blood test which will help us determine if you have a concussion."

"Okay, what were the three words I asked you to remember?"

Bea answered quickly, "Car, plate, banana. Now can I

go home?"

"We are going to wait for the blood tests to come back, but I think you may have experienced a slight concussion, even though you don't have the usual responses I would expect to find in my assessment. Since you did recently have a concussion though, I'd like to keep you here overnight to monitor you."

Pat Oakley and Dr. Vlk walked into the room just then. The small exam room became very crowded, so Christina stepped outside. Pat went over to Bea and gave her a kiss on the cheek. "How are you doing? The nurse said you got hit in the head. Are you okay?"

"I feel fine except for a little headache. Even that is getting better. Pat, tell them I can go home. I can't stay here while Claire is missing."

"Don't you think we should do what the doctor advises?"

Dr. Holiday turned to Christina. "You know her. Don't you think she should stay overnight for monitoring?"

"I agree with Dr. Holiday. Why don't we wait until the blood tests are back and then decide? If the tests are good, and you don't feel any worse, we can discuss it further. Dr. Holiday is an excellent doctor and you can trust his decision. Bea, Pat, I'll be out in the waiting room if you have any further questions. Doctor Holiday, may I talk with you outside?"

Stepping outside the cubicle and down the hall, Christina asked quietly, "How did the concussion assessment go?"

"She passed with flying colors. She stumbled a little, but quickly regained her balance. I still think she should stay for observation."

"I understand, and normally I would agree with you. Her foster child was just kidnapped by the man who hit her and she wants to go home. I really think it would ease her mind to be among her usual settings and among her loved ones. If the Brain Trauma Indicator test comes back and doesn't show any elevated protein levels, I think you can let her go home. Her husband will take care of her and I will stop in to monitor her."

"Okay. The blood test is very new and I'm not sure how well it works, but I will trust your expertise. You know her and know what kind of patient she is. If you think she will behave and rest, then she can be released...IF the test is clear. I'll check in with her after the test comes back."

***

Bea was restlessly sitting on the edge of the bed and she kept glancing at the clock on the wall. Her head had been cleaned and bandaged and she had removed the hospital gown and put on her regular clothes. There was still some blood on the neck and shoulder of her blouse, but she didn't seem to mind.

"When are we getting out of here? It's been hours."

"It has only been an hour since they drew your blood. You know you aren't the only patient in the hospital who needs their blood evaluated."

"I know." Sigh. "I just can't rest while poor Claire is out there with that horrible man. Why would he come and take her away?"

"You will never understand people who do such evil things, because you don't have an evil bone in your body. I'd like to think that somewhere, sometime in his life he must have been terribly hurt to become so cruel. But I also think some people just have something broken from birth. Maybe it's lack of love or maybe it's genetic. Smarter men then me haven't figured it out and neither can I."

They turned toward the door as Doctor Holiday walked in. "I'm sorry to have had you wait so long, but your blood test is back. It is clear, so, while I would rather you stay overnight, if you insist on going home, you can."

"Oh, thank you!"

"Just a minute. There are some things you need to do if I release you. First, you cannot be alone for at least forty-eight hours. If there are ANY changes, you need to come back in. No, sports for at least a week."

"No chance of that Doctor. If we have to tie her to the bed, she is going to rest."

"What about swimming? I love to swim."

"You will have to do without it for at least a week. You should be resting and healing. No doing anything that might risk a fall. Get all the sleep you can. Your body needs rest to heal. Most of all, avoid stress. It puts a tremendous amount of strain on our bodies. Remember, this is not your first head injury. Each one increases the risk of permanent damage."

"I promise to try. The stress part might be hard right now, but I will pray for serenity."

Both Pat and Bea gave each other dubious looks. It would be hard to relax until Claire was safe.

"Okay then, it was nice to meet you both. The nurse will be in with some paperwork and some aftercare instructions. Please make an appointment with your family doctor within the next week.

51

Brad knuckles were white as he grabbed on to the steering wheel of his car. He kept glancing right and left as he swerved around cars and sped up Highway 1 toward Moss Landing. Usually he enjoyed this stretch of highway with its sand dunes, artichoke and strawberry fields, but today he barely noticed them.

I'd bet anything that he is going to try and escape in his boat. If I can get there fast enough, I may be able to stop him. Come on, come on, get out of my way! Can't you see the light on the top of my car?

Brad pounded on the steering wheel with his fist as another tractor took it's time to pull to the side of the road. He took the left turn onto Moss Landing Road and then Sandholdt Road heading toward the harbor. His car kicked up a storm of sand that had drifted over the road since the last storm, and skidded a little before he got it back under control.

Pulling up to the Harbormaster's building, Brad jumped out of the car with his gun drawn. He saw the white mustang sitting in the parking lot and felt the hood with one hand, while keeping his gun and eyes trained forward.

He looked in the car windows in the hope that he may have left Claire in the car. It was empty except for empty bottle, coffee cups and fast food wrappers.

Still warm. He must have gotten here a few minutes ago.

Brad cautiously moved around the car and toward the boats moored at the dock. Whale Watch Excursion and Elkhorn Slough Tour boats were coming in after an afternoon of cruising. Otherwise, nothing was moving. The normally locked gate to the dock was open and Brad moved slowly from boat to boat, with his gun drawn and his eyes open for any movement. There was one man working on his boat who looked up worriedly when he saw Brad.

Brad lowered his gun and pulled out his badge and ID. "Don't worry, I am a police officer. Did you happen to see a tall man with pock marks on his face and a small, blond girl today?"

"Yeah, they came by here and got on their boat and headed out to sea. He seemed to be in a big hurry. He almost ran into one of the tour boats that were coming in to the dock. He definitely didn't follow the speed limit for inside the harbor."

"How long ago was this?"

"Oh, maybe a half hour ago."

Brad put away his gun. "Can you tell me what kind of boat he has and the name, if any on it?

"It was a beauty. A Back Cove 32. Full out it goes about 25 plus knots. I didn't see a name on it, but the owner fit your description. They thought it was a secret, but everyone here knew that he had been shacking up with Gladys in the Harbormasters cabin. It was sad to hear she was dead. Do you think he had anything to do with it?"

"I can't discuss and ongoing investigation. What color was his boat?"

"It had a white bottom and a wood upper deck and an inboard motor.

"Thanks, you've been a big help."

Brad turned away and got the Coast Guard on the phone.

"This is Detective Brad Evans of the Monterey Police Department. May I talk to Commander Sutton. It's urgent."

"Yes, Sir. I will get him right away."

"This is Chief Sutton. I didn't expect to hear from you again so soon, Detective. How can I help?"

"We need an assist with a water pursuit. The man we believe has committed at least two murders, has left town in a boat. We suspect he killed the woman you found recently and his wife. This time he has also kidnapped a child and we think he plans on killing her as well. Can you help us?"

"Of course. What kind of boat are we looking for?"

"It's a Back Cove 32. White with a wood grain top deck. The owners name is Eliott James. The child's name is Claire. Be careful, he is armed and very dangerous."

"Our men are trained to apprehend armed suspects. We'll get him for you. Did he leave from Monterey?"

"No, from Moss Landing. I'm there now, but will return to Monterey immediately. We don't know which direction he was headed when he got into open water."

"That's a powerful boat, but ours are even more so. We'll get him for you. I'll request an aerial assist to locate him. It will come from our San Francisco station, but should be here before he gets too far."

"Thanks. Do whatever you can to save the little girl."

"We will. Take care and I'll see you soon."

52

As Brad arrived in Monterey, he could hear the Coast Guard helicopter going back and forth, searching for Elliot James' boat. He pulled up to the gate of the Coast guard station on Lighthouse and showed his ID before being allowed to enter. Parking the car, he entered the small building and checked in with the person on duty.

"Just a minute. Chief Sutton is expecting you." The duty officer made a brief phone call and turned to Brad.

"Please follow me, Detective. I will take you to the Chief."

Walking down a short hall, they knocked and then entered Chief Sutton's office. The Chief was about the same age as Brad, lean and straight-backed. He was wearing Navy Blue pants and shirt and a baseball cap with the Coast Guard insignia on it. His shirt had his name and insignia. His black boots had water stains on then from hours on the water. He was friendly but wore an aura of efficiency and control.

Rising from his desk and extending his hand to Brad, he said, "Welcome Detective. We have a helicopter flying a grid over the Bay to find your suspect. He did not see him anywhere north of the bay so we expect he is heading south. We should have a sighting soon. Our men are ready to go after him as soon as we have a location. You are welcome to stay here as long as you want, or you can join us on the ship."

"Thank you, sir. If you don't mind, I would like to accompany you onboard. I'll just tell my Chief what is going on.?"

"Sure, and don't call me Sir. Ray is fine."

"Thanks, you can call me Brad."

Chief Sutton turned to his aide. "Please take the Detective to the galley for a cup of coffee while he waits."

"I will tell you as soon as we know anything."

Brad was starting to leave when the phone rang. He paused and Chief Sutton waved at him to wait. He listened for a minute and then hung up.

"The helicopter found the boat. He is heading out to sea and near Lovers Point in Pacific Grove. The helicopter will follow him until we approach, but there is a storm coming and heavy fog rolling in. He will have to turn back to base soon."

"Let's go. The men are waiting for me on the boat."

53

It was a short walk across Foam Street and down to the harbor. Chief Sutton led Brad to a 45-foot grey boat with the distinctive red, white and blue slash of color on the bow. There was a big orange-red fender running around the entire boat. As they climbed aboard, Brad could see two bigger boats in the neighboring slips. Ray saw him looking and said, "This size boat is considered a medium response boat. It is what we normally use in this type of situation. We use it in search and rescue, ports, waterways and coastal security; law enforcement; and drug and migrant interdiction. It travels faster than some of our older boats."

"How fast can it go?"

"Her maximum speed is 42.5 knots. Much faster than the boat you said the suspect is in. We shouldn't have any trouble catching up to him."

Handing Brad a life vest and helmet, he said, "You will have to stay in the pilothouse, but I want you to wear these as a safety precaution. Our people have floatation suits they wear in case anyone goes overboard."

Brad sat in one of the four seats in the pilothouse and looked around as they left the harbor. There were gun mounts fore and aft of the boat and recovery platforms on three sides. A large light was attached to the pilot house and several antennas.

As they left the harbor behind, the boat picked up speed in the bay. Brad could see the fog rolling in and whitecaps forming. Despite the rocky water he was fairly comfortable in his seat.

"I thought it would be rougher, considering the waves that are forming."

"In the old boats it would have been, but these boats have shock-mitigating seats for crew comfort. It also helps with endurance if we are out for a long time. I forgot to ask; do you get seasick?"

"Not yet. I've lived near the water my whole life and used to sail. I'd like to get back to it, but there never seems to be enough time."

"I know what you mean."

The pilot turned to face the men behind him. "Chief, I have the suspect's boat in sight. We should catch up to him in a few minutes."

They heard the helicopter turning around and heading back to his base in San Francisco. As promised, they were withing yards of James' boat in minutes.

Chief Sutton got on the bull horn. "Elliot James, this is the United States Coast Guard. Stop your boat and prepare for boarding."

James turned his head to look at them but sped up to try to outrun them.

"This is the United States Coast Guard. Stop your boat now or we will fire."

James reached down and grabbed Claire. He hugged her close to his chest as the boat continued on. The waves were even bigger than before and the wind was picking up. James was having trouble steering the boat while holding on to her. They staggered back and forth as the boat moved over the waves.

Realizing that he would not be able to out run the bigger boat, he turned and threw Claire overboard into the waves. Then he powered on without even looking behind him.

That should divert their attention long enough for me to get away. In this fog, they will have a hard time finding me.

"Oh no! He threw Claire overboard. Do something! Save her!" Brad rushed down the stairs and onto the deck all the while trying to keep an eye on the girl struggling in the waves. She would be visible for a moment and then slip out of sight with the next swell.

"Brad, get back in the pilothouse. You will only be in the way down here. My men and women are trained to do water rescues. They'll get her, don't worry."

Reluctantly, Brad returned to the pilothouse but his stomach churned with anxiety.

The Coast Guard boat had already moved in closer to the child. She was getting visibly weaker as she struggled to stay afloat in the heavy surf and strong winds. They pulled alongside her and tossed a life preserver for her to grab. She tried, but a wave swept it away. They tried again and this time, she was able to hold on. The boat was in idle and they were trying to get her on the port recovery platform. A huge wave hit the side of the boat and washed her away. Luckily, she managed to hold onto the life preserver, although she was spitting water. The crew moved down the length of the boat and managed to pull her up onto the aft platform. They quickly pulled her aboard and wrapped her in an aluminum blanket to warm her.

Brad was dying to go down and meet her but he knew that it was dangerous in the rough weather. Within minutes she was brought up to him and rushed into his arms.

"Uncle Brad! Oh, I am so glad to see you. I knew you would save me! My father said he wanted to kill me and leave me far out at sea for the fish to eat!"

"It's okay now darling. He won't hurt you. You are with me. It is the Coast Guard sailors you should thank. Without them he would have gotten away."

"Chief, can you still catch him?"

"We could if we knew where he was going, but in this fog, he could be anywhere. I wouldn't worry though. The thing about boats is that they can't stay out at sea forever. Eventually, he will have to find a harbor for gas, food and water. When he does, we will get him. I've sent a bulletin out alerting everyone to be on the lookout for him and his boat. In this weather he better be a good sailor or he will crash before he makes it into a harbor."

Looking at Claire he asked, "How are you doing little lady?"

Claire looked shyly up from where she was nestled in Brad's arms and said, "Thank you for saving me. He is a mean, mean man."

"You are very welcome. Let's get a life vest on you. We should be back in the harbor soon, but the water is very rough and I wouldn't want you to get hurt."

Within minutes they had reached the harbor and were back in their berth. After Claire climbed down from the pilothouse, she went up to each of the sailors and hugged them as she thanked them. Although trying to look like it was just part of the job, each of them smiled with pride at what they had accomplished.

Brad shook Chief Sutton's hand. "Thank you so much. I owe you one. I hope we can get James as well, but just having Claire back safe and sound is enough for now."

"The way she ran into your arms I gathered she was more to you than just a random child."

"She definitely is. My sister found her when she was abandoned by her father and has been a foster mother to her since then. We have all grown very fond of her."

"Well, I'm glad we were able to help. I'm sure James will turn up and we will get him to pay for this and everything else he has done. Keep in touch."

54

Brad drove Claire back to Bea's house. It was a short drive through the streets of Monterey to where they lived.

"Before we get home, I wanted to ask you something. Is that okay?"

Claire nodded.

"When did you start talking? I was really surprised to hear you talking to the Chief."

"I don't know." She said with a shrug. "When my dad stole me from Bea, the words just started to come out. I guess it was because I wasn't afraid. Well, I was afraid, but not of talking. I told him you would get me back."

"Well, I had a lot of help from the Coast Guard." He reached over to tussle her wet hair. "We'll be home in a minute and we'll get you into warm clothes. Bea and Pat are going to be awfully happy to have you back. They have been very worried."

"How is Bea? My daddy hit her really hard."

"She is fine. She had a little cut on her head but nothing serious. She is at home waiting to hear that we found you."

"Brad, is my dad going to come back again? I don't want to be with him."

"I wouldn't worry about that, darling. There are a lot of people looking for him and when they find him, he is going to jail for a long, long time."

Pulling up into the Oakley driveway, Brad had to put a hand on Claire so she wouldn't jump out of the car before he stopped. When he finally removed her seatbelt, she jumped out and ran to the door, dropping her blanket on the way. The door was locked and she rang the doorbell over and over and pounded on the door. Pat threw open the door and Claire jumped into his arms, making him step back a couple of paces to keep his balance.

"Claire! Oh sweety, we are so happy you are back. Let's go see Bea, but don't jump on her like you did to me. We don't want to knock her over again."

Pat put down Claire and turned to talk to Brad. "You go on ahead baby; I'll be right there. Bea is in the kitchen."

Pat grasped Brad's arm in a warm handshake. "Thank you for bringing her home. I thought we'd never see her again. Did you get her father too?"

"No, unfortunately he got away. The Coast Guard is confident they will get him though. I'll tell you all about it when we are with Bea."

The men walked into the kitchen where Claire was wrapped around Bea's legs. "Pat, did you know that Claire can talk? Say something to him, sweety."

"Hi Pat. I'm so happy to be back here! I thought I'd never see you again." Claire shivered.

"Come on. Let's get you out of these wet clothes and then we can talk all about it. Pat, would you make some hot chocolate for Claire?"

"Sure, what about you, Brad? Hot chocolate or coffee?"

"Whatever you have ready. It was pretty cold on the coat with the fog and storm. I have to call in to the office. I also want Christina to come over and check her out. I think she is okay, but we need to be sure."

Brad pulled out his cell phone to make the calls and then settled down at the table. "Thanks, Pat. When Bea gets back, I will give you the story and then I have to get back and file a report. Christina is going to stop by after work."

Bea and Claire entered the kitchen and joined Pat and Brad at the table.

"I can't believe what a little magpie our Claire has become. It is so good to hear her talking. She told me a little bit about what happened after they left here, but I'd like to hear Brad's story too."

"Well, after I left here, I drove to Moss Landing. I was hoping I could get there before he left. I had a hunch he would take off on his boat, and I was right. I missed him by less than a half hour. When I realized he was on the water already, I called the Coast Guard and asked them to assist me in apprehending him. We weren't sure which direction he may have gone, so they called out a helicopter to locate his boat. I had just arrived back in Monterey and arrived at the Coast Guard Station when they got word that the helicopter had located him and he wasn't too far away. The Coast Guard launched a boat and we were able to cut him off. When they told him to surrender, he threw Claire overboard and took off. We had to save her, so he was able to get away. Because of the storm and heavy fog, the helicopter had already left, so we didn't know where to follow. They put out bulletins all up and down the coast, so I am confident they will find him."

"Wow, that's some story. I'm so glad you were able to get her back, even if you didn't catch her father. Claire can fill me in on her part of the story later."

"Thanks, Pat. I better get going. I need to fill out a report and touch base with Chief Sutton again. Can you bring her down to the station tomorrow so we can fill in what happened to her after he took her?"

Pat nodded that he would bring her over and clapped

Brad on the shoulder. Giving Claire a hug, Brad let himself out.

"Well Claire, I think there is one more person who would want to see you." Pat went to the back door and let Blaze into the house. He ran right over to Claire, who had jumped off her chair when she saw him. He put his paws on her shoulders and began licking her face.

Giggling, Claire said, "Blaze, oh what a good boy. Have you been keeping watch on the house?" She put her arms around his neck and hugged him tightly until he began to squirm. The doorbell rang and Blaze took off for the door, hackles up and barking ferociously.

Pat went to door and grabbed his collar. "Down boy. Sit. Good Boy." Opening the door, he saw Christina carrying her medical bag. Blaze immediately started to wag his tail so hard that his whole body was swinging back and forth. Christina reached down to pet him.

"Hi Blaze, Hi Pat. I hear we have some good news."

"Sure, come into the kitchen. We are all having so hot chocolate. Would you like a cup?"

"That sounds great, but maybe after I look at Claire. I'm surprised Brad didn't just bring her to the hospital."

"I think he was trying to save us some money. We've been keeping CHOMP pretty busy these last few months."

"Hi Claire, would you mind if I take a look at you? I want to make sure you don't have any serious injuries."

"Alright. I'm okay though. Brad saved me before my dad really hurt me."

Christina looked at Bea and Pat in astonishment. "When did she start talking?"

"Just since she was kidnapped. I guess it snapped something that was holding her back."

Christina listened to her chest and checked out the bruises on her face where James had slapped her. "Well, aside from a few bruises, she looks great. This is one sturdy girl. You can put some ice on her bruises if they bother her, but they will fade on their own."

"Boy listen to that wind blowing! There were branches down all over the road when I was driving over here. It's a good thing they got Claire off the water before this storm really got going. I wouldn't want to be out there now."

"Christina, I'm sorry that Brad isn't here right now, but he had to get back and file a report on what happened today. Join us for some hot chocolate though."

"I'd like to, but I better get back. It's been a long day at work and I'm pretty tired. Thanks anyway."

As Christina opened the front door, it blew out of her hands from a sudden gust of wind. Rain was falling like a sheet, blocking her view.

"Wow, it's really nasty outside. Are you sure you don't want to stay awhile and see if it calms down?"

"The weather report said it would only get worse in the evening. I better get home and make sure I didn't leave any windows open."

"I'll see you all soon. I'm so happy for you that Claire is home safe and sound."

55

Brad was filling out forms to report what happened. *Boy, what a day. First James broke into the house and hit Bea. Then he kidnapped Claire. I followed him to Moss Landing and then back again to Monterey to the Coast Guard Station. We found his boat, but lost him again when he tossed Claire overboard. Now this terrible storm has stopped us from trying to find James and bring him to justice, I'll just hope that Chief Sutton is right and he will turn up again and we can capture him.*

Brad took his report over to Chief Eddie Murphy. He knocked on the window and the Chief motioned him in.

"I finished my report on today's events. I'm sorry to say, we didn't catch Eliott James, but we were able to save the child before he did anything to her. She is coming in tomorrow to fill out her report."

"I'm glad the child is safe. I thought you said she doesn't talk."

"She didn't. The doctors felt it was because of her original trauma and, whatever happened today, reversed that."

"That's good. Besides today's kidnapping, I want to hear if she knows anything about the death of her mother. Now, I have a bone to pick with you. You should not have gone after James by yourself. What if you had caught him in Moss Landing? You had no backup. This could have ended very badly. You're lucky he was already gone. We already have one officer on the injured list. We can't afford to lose another."

"Yes sir. I understand, sir. I knew he had a lead on us and wanted to follow quickly."

"No excuses, Evans. I don't want to have this happen again."

Looking contrite, Brad said, "Yes, sir."

"Now get out of here. With the way this storm is building, it may end up being a busy night for us."

Brad knew he was lucky to get off with just a reprimand. *He's right. It was a risky thing to go after him by myself. That wind is fierce! I better get out of here before I get called into a weather disaster.*

The lights in the building flickered and then went off. Within seconds, the generator kicked in and the lights came back on and you could hear computers beeping and reloading. Brad hurried outside and fought through the wind and rain to his car.

He gave a quick call to Christina to see if she had been to see Claire.

"How is she?"

"Amazingly good. I was worried she might have swallowed water, but her lungs were clear. Aside from a few bruises, he didn't do any serious damage."

"That's great to hear. Where are you now? Are you still at Bea's?"

"No, I left a little while ago. I am at home now. I wanted to get back before the storm got any worse. Do you want to come over? I would enjoy the company. The way the wind is whipping the trees around has me a little freaked out."

"I was hoping you would ask. How about if I stop at Gianni's and bring a pizza?"

"Perfect. I'll have a bottle of red wine open. Just come on in."

***

By the time Brad got to the front door of Christina's house, the pizza box was covered with water from the rain. He opened the door and tipped the box to pour off the water onto the stoop. He put the box down on the table and shook out his umbrella and coat.

"Hello. I'm here!"

"I'm in the kitchen. Come on in. Boy, look what the cat dragged in! Give me the box and I'll get it ready while you go into the bathroom and towel off. You can use the hair dryer too, if you want."

"Thanks, I feel like I swam from the car to your house. What a storm. We usually don't get them this bad in December. I hope this means its going to be a wet winter and we can end the drought."

Brad dried himself off and put on sweats he had left at Christina's house on a previous visit. As he walked into the kitchen again, he could smell the warm pizza that she was cutting into slices. She had put candles on the dining table and the fireplace in the living room was oblazing. The warm crackling of the fire, the soft lighting and the delicious pizza smells made him appreciate the cozy atmosphere she had created.

Brad went up, lifted her long, blond hair, and kissed her on the neck. "You smell great."

"Are you sure it's me or the pizza you're smelling?"

"Now that you mention it; it probably is the pizza."

Christina playfully flicked him with a kitchen towel. "Well, you better sit down then before the pizza gets cold."

Brad helped her carry the plates and pizza out to the

table. Then he pulled out her chair for her to sit. He reached over to grab a slice and took a big bite off the end. "Oh man, that is so good. I was worried that it got waterlogged from the rain. I forgot to ask what kind of topping you wanted to I just did an 'everything' pizza. You can take off what you don't like."

"You lucky man, I like 'everything'!"

There was a pop, and the electricity went out. Unlike the police station, Christina didn't have a generator.

"Thank goodness you have the candles and fire going. I kind of like it this way. Very cozy."

Putting her hand over his she replied, "Yes, it is. At least until it starts to get cold. Hopefully it won't last long."

"How would you like a generator for Christmas? I'm sure there will be other storms and it will come in handy."

"Oh no, that's too much. I'll get my own generator, but you can help me pick one out."

After they finished the pizza, they took their wine glasses and sat on the couch in front of the fire with a quilt around their shoulders. Chatting quietly, they listened to the wind howling and the rain hitting the windows. Christina and Brad talked about their days and then sat quietly gazing at the fire dancing in the fireplace. Christina's head was on his shoulder and his arm was around her. Brad was filled with a feeling of peace and contentment. He leaned over to kiss Christina and realized she had fallen asleep. He carefully pulled his arm from around her, got up, laid her down on the couch while tucking the covers around her shoulders. Walking around the house he made sure that all the candles were out. He put another log on the fire and grabbed a quilt off the bed before sitting down in one of the chairs where he could watch the light dancing across her tranquil face.

56

B rad sat at his desk and remembered the warm feeling of the night before. The storm had passed through, and except for broken branches and trees, one would never know how awful it was the night before. The sun was shining and it was a balmy seventy degrees outside. The sky was blue without a cloud in the sky.

His ringing phone brought him out of his reverie.

"Detective Evans, how may I help you?"

"Hi Brad, it's Ray Sutton over at the Coast Guard Station. I've got some good news for you. A tourist was out walking this morning and saw a body on the beach near Asilomar. We retrieved the body and it appears to be the man you have been looking for. He is pretty beat up from the waves and rocks, but he definitely fits the description you gave us. We have a call into the Sheriff's office to pick him up, but I thought you'd want to see him first.

"You bet! I'll just check in with my Chief and I will be right over."

Brad walked over to Chief Murphy's office and knocked. The Chief waved him in.

"I just got a call from the Coast Guard that a body matching James was found on Asilomar beach. I'd like to go over and check it out."

"I hope it's him and this will put an end to this case. I like it when we don't have to go to trial."

"Yes sir, I understand. I can't wait to have him put safely away, one way or the other."

"Okay, get out of here. I hope you come back with good news."

Brad met Chief Sutton in the Station parking lot and he walked him down the hall to a room where they were holding the body until the Sheriff came to take him to the morgue.

They paused at the table for a minute and then the Chief pulled back the tarp that was covering the body.

Brad looked at him for a moment and noticed the bruises, cuts and abrasions on his face and body. His features were devoid of color and he had a waxen look to him. *He looks like a rescue dummy. I guess, without the spirit within each of us, really, we are just a shell. I know I should be happy he is dead, but I just feel sad. No one is born bad; I wonder what happened that soured his life?*

"Yes, that's him. It looks like he had a rough time before he washed up. Did you find the boat?"

"That storm last night was pretty brutal. If he was in the surf for very long, he would have had quite a struggle to survive. We don't have any sign of the boat yet. It may have capsized and sunk in the storm or it may have broken up on the rocks. Then again, he may have been washed overboard and the boat it is floating somewhere in the ocean. I'd like to think it will show up, but sometimes they don't. After the Tsunami in Japan there was a boat that sailed all the way across the Pacific by itself with no crew on board. There was another ship that had been sailing between Greece and Haiti in 2018. It ran into trouble and the Coast Guard rescued the crew. The ship somehow got lost and showed up two years later on the coast of Ireland. Hurricane Dennis washed it up on the rocks of the south shore."

"That's an amazing story. I'm just glad we found his body. After what he has put our family through, it's good to know we can finally breathe again. I better get going, there is someone I have to see. I'll let the coroner take it from here. I really appreciate all your help with this." Shaking the Chief's hand, Brad walked down the corridor toward his car. The beautiful Monterey sunshine couldn't compare to the feeling of relief that he felt.

***

Brad pulled up to a small apartment complex on the edge of town, on the border between Monterey and Sand City. He went down the cement sidewalk to one of the non-descript doors.

Brad's knock was opened within second's by Sue Blake. "Hi, Sue. I didn't expect to see you here. How's he doing?"

"I have the day off, so I came over here. He's actually doing much better than they had anticipated. He still gets headaches and he can be a little unsteady on his feet, but he is doing more and more. Come on it. He'll be happy to see you."

Brad wiped his feet on the mat and walked into a small living room and approached a recliner where Tom Kent was watching a soccer match. A twinge of guilt flooded him as he saw the young man, obviously in pain. He was pale and had lost a lot of weight since he was hurt. When he saw Brad, Tom tried to stand up, but Brad stopped him. "Hey, no need to get up. This isn't a formal visit. I'm sorry I haven't been by sooner, but Eliott James has been keeping us very busy."

Tom turned off the television and reached out a hand to Brad. "It's just good to see you. Christina has been keeping us up on the latest news. How is Bea doing? I hear that beast knocked her out again and stole Claire away."

"She's fine, she needed a couple of stitches on her

head and she is aggravated that they had to cut away some of her hair, but she will be okay. What is it with women and their hair? I think she is more upset about that than her injury."

"I have some good news for you. After James attacked Bea and took Claire, I followed him out to the Marina in Moss Landing. I was too late to catch him out there, but I was able to notify the Coast Guard and they sent out a helicopter to find him. We cut off his boat and almost had him, but he threw Claire overboard and we had to stop to save her. We got her, but he had disappeared in the fog. Because of the storm, we had to turn around."

"Is Claire alright? Poor kid. She'll never be safe until he is captured. I can't wait to see him pay for all he has done."

Sue came over and put a soothing hand on Tom's shoulder. "Besides Bea and Claire, we almost lost Tom to that monster."

Reaching up to hold her hand, Tom said, "Hey, it's part of the job. I'm getting better every day. It takes more than a little blow on the head to keep me down."

"Claire is doing fine too. You wouldn't believe what a chatterbox she has become. If the trauma of her being abandoned took her voice, the shock of seeing him again seems to have loosened her tongue. The good thing is that we don't have to worry about Eliott James anymore! The Coast Guard retrieved a body this morning and it was James. He was pretty beat up from the storm and rocks, but I was able to make a positive ID."

"Oh man, oh man, oh man, I can't believe it. Thank you so much Brad. That's the best medicine a man can have."

"Hey, I didn't do anything. The good old Monterey Bay delivered him to us. Well, I wanted to give you the good news myself, but I better get back to the station. Claire is coming in today to give her statement."

Sue came around and gave Brad a big hug and Tom clasped his hand in a strong handshake. As Sue walked him back to the door, she gave him another hug and a kiss on the cheek. "Thank you for coming. This is what he needed to hear to give him the incentive to get better. He has been upset that he is laid up and can't help."

57

After lunch, Brad was getting a cup of coffee when Claire and Bea were brought to his desk by a police officer. Hugging the two of them, he led them over to an interrogation room where they could talk in quiet.

"Now, Claire, I just need to have you tell me in your own words what happened after you left Bea's house. Don't be worried if you can't remember something, or it isn't in order. We can straighten it out afterwards." Taking out a recording device, he placed it on his desk in front of Claire.

Bea patted the girl's hand. "Go ahead honey, I'm right here. There's nothing to be afraid of."

In a soft voice Claire said, "Well, after Man knocked out Bea and tied her up, he dragged me to the car. I thought he had killed her." Claire wiped the tears from her eyes. "When I tried to run away, he hit me and threw me in the front seat. Then we drove to his boat and he forced me on board. I tried to get away, but he hit me again. Really hard." Bea looked worriedly at Brad.

"Go on sweety. He can't hurt you anymore."

"On the boat, he had me sit in a chair right next to

him. Whenever I tried to get up, he grabbed my arm and forced me back in the seat. He said that he'd tie me down if I didn't sit still. I didn't want that because, I knew I'd never be able to get away if he did. We sailed for a long time and the waves were getting higher and higher. I had a hard time to not fall over. Then we heard the other big boat call his name and tell us to stop. He swore a lot then and got out his gun. I thought he was going to shoot me! Instead, he took me to the edge and threw me overboard. Mama taught me to swim, so I tried to stay afloat until the sailors threw me a buoy. When they pulled me onboard, I saw Uncle Brad. I guess that's it."

"You did fine. If you think of anything else, you can call me. Okay? You are a very brave girl. I'm very proud of you."

"Bea, we got your testimony at the hospital. Is there anything you want to add?"

"No, it was pretty fast. He came in, grabbed Claire and knocked me out before tying me up. I remember trying to get out of the restraints when Mrs. Collett came to the door and called 911. She untied me, but I was bleeding a lot from the cut on my head. Head wounds always bleed a lot, but it wasn't as bad as it looked. After they sewed me up, I went home."

Putting her arm around Claire and drawing her close, she added, "I wasn't worried about me, but I was scared to death that he would hurt her. I'm so glad she is back with us again."

"Now, Claire, I know we have been calling you Claire because we didn't know your real name. Can you tell me what it is so I can put it on the report?"

"My mama called me Jessica, but I like Claire better."

"Okay then, I'll put Jessica on the report, but I think you deserve to pick your own name for your new life of freedom. What do you think, Bea?"

"I think that's a great idea. I'll call social services and tell them that our Jane Doe finally has a real name."

"Brad, why don't you come over tonight for a little celebration. Bring Christina too."

"I'd love that. What time?"

"Whenever you can. I have a stew in the crock pot, so we can eat anytime. Just give me a call when you know when you are both coming."

"Will do. I'll see you later."

58

Parking in the driveway at the Oakley house, Brad ran around and opened the door for Christina.

"My, my, what a gentleman."

He opened the back door and pulled out a big teddy bear that was almost as tall as he was.

"Where did you get that? It's huge!"

"I drove over to Costco and picked it up. I figure a big event deserves a big gift."

"Well, it certainly is big. How do you expect a little girl like, Claire to carry that around? You can barely handle it yourself."

"Hmm, I hadn't thought of that. I guess we will just have to see. Help guide me so I don't trip over something. I can barely see around it."

Pat heard the car in the driveway and opened the door. Laughing at the huge bear, he ushered them in the house. Blaze barked when they came in but backed away when he saw the huge teddy bear. He tilted his head from side to side as if he was unsure what to do. Brad put the bear on the floor and called to the dog.

"Come here Blaze. Come on. There's nothing to be afraid of." Petting the hesitant dog, Brad put one paw of the toy out so Blaze could sniff it. "See boy, it's not real. It won't hurt anyone."

Blaze took one more sniff and walked away with his head high. "If he were a person, I'd say he was trying to convince us that he hadn't been afraid!"

Claire came rushing into the hallway and skidded to a stop. "Is that for me?"

When Brad nodded, she took a running leap and landed on the bear. Hugging it for dear life, she started dragging it into the family room. "Thanks, Uncle Brad. This is the best!"

Following her into the back of the house, they saw the Oakley boys and Bea, sitting on the couch. The boys got up and offered their seat to Brad, Christina and Pat.

"What are you all drinking? Can I have a beer? How about you Christina?"

"Is that wine you are drinking, Bea? I'll have some of that."

Claire was cuddled up in her big bear and the boys had settled into a couple of the comfy chairs in front of the fireplace.

"Dinner is ready anytime we are, but I wanted to

talk about Christmas. It seems like a year ago we were all gathered for Thanksgiving. So much has happened since then. Some of it bad, but some of it was wonderful". Bea glanced over at Claire.

"I'd like to have everyone here again for Christmas. I'm still a little shaky, so I'd like each of you to bring something. Pat and I will provide the drinks and a ham. The rest of you can decide what you would like to add. Brad, do you think Tom and Sue can come? I haven't seen him since his injury and I want him to know he is family. Boys, you can invite the girls too. I want it to be a big celebration of new life."

Everyone began chatting about what they would bring as they headed into the dining room.

Claire looked around the side of her big teddy and felt peace and stillness filling her as she looked around at all these loving people.

59

The Christmas tree shimmered in the corner of the living room. Multicolored strands of lights circled the tree while colored balls and homemade ornaments reflected the glow. Underneath, the floor was scattered with an array of boxes, wrapping paper and ribbons. Everyone was still in their pajamas with messy bed heads. Claire played with a doll that looked like her, with blond hair and blue eyes. The boys were playing on new hand-held electrical gadgets. Even Blaze was chewing on a new squeaky toy. Bea and Pat were wrapped in cozy bathrobes, looking at their children and sipping a cup of warm coffee as they watched them happily at play. Pat put his arm around Bea and kissed her on the head.

"Having a young child with us sure got us all out of bed earlier than usual. I don't regret it though. When I see the happiness on her face, it makes it all worth it. However, a cup of coffee was the best present I received."

Bea poked him in the ribs. "So, you didn't like the new drone I bought for you or the gifts from the kids?"

"Sorry, that was my lack of sleep talking. Of course, I loved your gifts." He gave Bea another kiss. "I think this is one of the best Christmas' we have ever had. Sometimes, it takes almost losing someone to make you realize how blessed you are. Everyone is safe and all the wounds are healing. While they are nice, the gifts feel less important."

"When should we tell Claire about our conversation with Mrs. West?

"Not yet. I want her to enjoy Christmas without thinking about anything else.

The doorbell rang and Claire jumped up to answer it. "Claire! Wait for one of us. We still don't want you opening the door by yourself."

"But, it's probably Uncle Brad and Christina!"

"I know, but it is a good habit for you to get into."

Wally hopped up and went with Claire to open the door.

"Merry Christmas, Claire, Wally. Help me carry some of these gifts, would you?"

Jumping with excitement Claire said, "Merry Christmas Uncle Brad. Merry Christmas, Christina. Come and see what Santa Claus brought me!"

She grabbed Brad and Christina's hands and pulled them into the family room. "Would you like a cookie? I made them myself. See? Some of the are trees and some are bells or stars. I put on the frosting and sprinkles."

"They look delicious, but I'll have one later."

"How about you Christina?"

Taking a cookie off the tray, Christina took a big bite. "Oh, these are so good. You must give me your recipe."

Claire giggled, "Oh Christina, they are just sugar cookies from a roll. I don't have a recipe. Maybe, when Bea is all well, we can learn to make other cookies."

Brad went over to talk to the boys and see what they were playing with. Christina went over to sit with Bea and Pat.

"Bea, the house looks beautiful. I don't know how you found the time to decorate with all that has been going on."

"I have to admit, that Pat did most of it...under my direction of course. Once Patty and Wally got home a couple of days ago and they helped set up the tree and hang the lights outside. It just wouldn't feel like Christmas without decorations. Besides, I wanted Claire to have a "real" Christmas. From what she has told me, they never celebrated it on the boat."

"She is such a sweet kid. Look at how much she is enjoying the gifts you gave her. I don't know how anyone could have treated her so badly. I am so happy that her, so called, father can't hurt her anymore. He might be her biological father, but he sure didn't know how a real father acts. All the men in this family would be better for her than he was."

"Thanks for the compliment, Christina. I had a loving, caring, father and I tried to be one to my boys. I was lucky to know Bea and Brad's parents, and they were also great role models. I can only believe that James must have had a terrible childhood to grow up the way he did. That doesn't excuse his behavior; many children from bad families grow up to be wonderful parents. From what Claire has told us, her mother was very good to her and tried to give her the love her father didn't. We hope that, being with us, helped her forget some of the nightmares she has endured."

Bea reached over and took Pat's hand. "I doubt if she can ever forget those memories, but I hope they will fade as she gets older."

"I don't want to be rude, Christina, but I better go get dressed. I know we are all family here, but I can't stay in my jammies all day."

"Go, go. I totally understand. Blaze and I are going to hang out and enjoy this tableau of Christmas joy you have created."

"Well, you can hang with Brad and Blaze, the rest of us need to get dressed. Wally, Patty, Claire, come on, it's time to get out of those pajamas and into some real clothes."

"Bea, can I wear the new sweater and tights I got from Santa Claus?"

"Of course, Claire. Bring them with you into your bedroom."

As Claire left, Blaze pulled away from Christina and followed the girl out of the room.

"Et tu, Blaze? I guess that just leaves us Brad."

They started to walk into the kitchen to get some coffee when Brad turned to her and gently brushed back a hair that had fallen in her face. Pulling her to him, he gave her a passionate kiss.

As they parted, he pointed to the mistletoe hanging over the doorframe.

"You don't need mistletoe to kiss me, but I'm glad you did."

Brad reached into his pocket and dropped to one knee. Holding out a box with a sparkling ring in it, he said, "Christina, I know we haven't been dating that long, but you are the best thing that has ever happened to me. You are good, and wise and put up with me, even when I am being a jerk. I can't imagine my life without you. Will you marry me?"

Christina's hand went to her mouth and she just stared at him for a minute with wide eyes. "Yes, oh yes! I never thought I'd ever meet a man like you. You fill my life with happiness, love and more than a little adventure. I would love to be your wife."

Brad rose and placed the ring on her finger and drew her into another passionate kiss. Just then, Wally walked in. "Get a room you two.

They drew apart, laughing, with their arms around each other's waists.

"Hey man, don't talk to my future wife like that!'

"What? Wife? You're kidding. When did that happen?"

"Just now. I waited until everyone was out of the room before I asked her. I didn't want to be embarrassed if she said no. You are the first one to know."

Bea walked in with Pat and Claire. "Know what?"

"Brad and Christina are engaged!"

"What? When? Oh, how wonderful! This is really something to celebrate."

Bea gave the couple hugs and held on to Brad a little longer as she whispered in his ear, "You'll pay for not telling your twin first."

Patty walked in and saw everyone beaming and hugging. "What did I miss? What's going on?"

Claire ran over and grabbed his hand, "Uncle Brad and Christina are going to get married!"

"What? You all knew? Why am I always the last to know everything? Congratulations you two. Let me give my new aunt-in-law a hug!"

The doorbell rang again and Bea went to open the door with Claire. "It's Tom and Sue! Merry Christmas. Come in, Come in. I am so glad you came."

"Thank you so much for inviting us. This is Tom's first outing since his surgery. We couldn't think of a better place to be on Christmas."

"Where do you want me to put these gifts, Bea?"

"Oh Tom, that wasn't necessary. We are just happy you are here."

"It's just some wine for you and a present for Claire. Since it is her first Christmas with you, I wanted to help make it memorable."

Blaze was aggressively sniffing at another package that Tom was holding. "Right, I forgot I also brought a little something for Blaze. Here you go, boy. Have at it."

Blaze took the bag from Tom and tore it open until several dog treats dropped out. The group barely noticed what they were before he gobbled them all up.

"The girl at the pet store said that dogs loved these homemade treats. I guess she was right!"

"Claire, you can open your gift now too."

Claire sat down on the floor and began gently unwrapping the present from Sue and Tom.

"Oh, oh! A horse! Look, Bea. It has a saddle and a brush for the mane and a halter and everything!" Hopping up, she gave the couple a hug and then ran into the kitchen to show the others.

"Look what Tom and Sue gave me! Isn't it cool?!"

After everyone admired her new toy, Claire ran back into the living room to play by the tree.

Brad shook Tom's hand and gave Sue a kiss on the cheek. "It's so good to see you both. How about a cup of coffee and some Danish?"

"That would be great. Do you mind if I sit down at the table? My legs are still a little weak after laying around for so long."

"That's a great idea. Our little kitchen isn't big enough for so many people. Wally, Patty, can you help bring everything to the table?"

Claire wandered back into the dining room with Blaze on her heels and her new horse in her hands.

Once everyone was settled, Bea looked at Pat. He nodded and began, "This is certainly a day of celebration and joy. We are surrounded by all the people we love and they are with the ones they love. Tom, you and Sue came last so you didn't hear the good news that Brad and Christina got engaged today."

"Hey, congratulations. Looks like we will both have a wedding to look forward to." Tom raised his coffee cup to salute the couple.

Once the chatter died down, Pat continued, "This year has been one filled with more than its share of adversity, but a lot of blessings as well. Come here Claire." The child crawled up onto Pat's lap. "Claire, are you happy here?"

"Oh yes. You are so good to me."

Pat and Bea looked at each other. "We have been talking to Mrs. West at the Children's Protective Services. Do you remember her?"

Claire nodded her head, but looked with apprehension at the adults. "Is everything okay?"

"Oh yes, don't worry. Anyway, we have been talking to her to see if we can have you stay here permanently. We would like to adopt you, if you would like that."

Bursting into tears, Claire buried her face in Pat's shoulder.

"What? What is it? Aren't you happy? I thought you liked it here."

"I, I do. I'm just so happy. I would love to stay here.

You are the best thing that has ever happened to me."

"Whew, for a minute, I was worried you were unhappy. Mrs. West still has to do a little research to see if your parents might have some other relatives that would like to take care of you. So far, they haven't found anyone and neither have the police. So, if nothing changes, we can go to court sometime next year and start the adoption process."

"Thank you, thank you. This is the best Christmas present of all!"

Author's Notes

Father Ramon Mestres: Father Mestres served as pastor at San Carlos Cathedral from 1893-1930. He married future President, Herbert Hoover, in a civil ceremony, to Lou Henry. Hoover was the first President of the USA to be married by a Catholic priest. Father Mestres also constructed the Lourdes Grotto and saved the Serra Oak Tree after it fell. He replanted it behind the church where it stayed until 1985. Perhaps, because of his long tenure and fondness for San Carlos, he decided to stay around in the afterlife. Monterey citizens have many stories of seeing his ghost around the parish.

The Sally P. Archer Child Advocacy Center and Bates-Eldredge Child Sexual Abuse Clinic for Monterey County is located at Natividad in the Barnet J. Segal Outpatient Center. Physicians perform medical-legal examinations to evaluate cases of suspected or actual child abuse to provide documented evidence to assist in the prosecution of criminal cases. It is the only service of its kind in Monterey County. You can contact the center at (831) 769-8682.

Mater Dolorosa,
Our Lady of Sorrows

Our Lady of Lourdes Grotto,
San Carlos Cathedral

Lighted Boat Parade

Dennis the Menace

House of the Four Winds

If you have enjoyed, *Silent Sorrow*, you might like to read, *The Cardinal in the Crypt*, the first book in the Cathedral Mysteries series. It is available at distribution sites online, or write Barbara at <u>CathedralMysteries@gmail.com</u>, for a signed copy.

Reader's comments are always appreciated.

Happy reading!

Barbara